Praise for *The Yellow Birds*

'A **masterpiece** of war literature and a classic.'
Hilary Mantel, *The Times* Books of the Year

'By turns shocking, philosophical,
frightening and elegiac.'
James Kidd, *Independent on Sunday*
Books of the Year

'One of the **best** war novels for years.'
John Burnside, *Scotsman*
Books of the Year

'The best novel I read this year was
The Yellow Birds. A **stunning** debut.'
Bob Johnston, *Irish Times*
Books of the Year

'In the great tradition of Hemingway and Tim O'Brien,
Kevin Powers's **exquisitely written** *The Yellow Birds*
draws us in to the combat zones of Iraq: the watch, the
alert ("Stay alive, Stay alert"), the bungle, the slaughter
and the irreparable aftermath.'
Edna O'Brien, *Guardian* Books of the Year

'A **vivid**, poetic account of modern warfare . . .
each line bleeds hard-fought truths.'
Richard Godwin, *Evening Standard*
Books of the Year

THE
YELLOW
BIRDS

KEVIN POWERS

SCEPTRE

First published in Great Britain in 2012 by Sceptre
An imprint of Hodder & Stoughton
An Hachette UK company

First published in paperback in 2013

1

A CIP catalogue record for this title is
available from the British Library

B format paperback ISBN 978 1 444 75614 2
A format paperback ISBN 978 1 444 76876 3
eBook ISBN 978 1 444 75616 6

Printed and bound by Clays Ltd, St Ives plc

Hodder & Stoughton policy is to use papers that are natural, renewable
and recyclable products and made from wood grown in sustainable forests.
The logging and manufacturing processes are expected to conform to the
environmental regulations of the country of origin.

Hodder & Stoughton Ltd
338 Euston Road
London NW1 3BH

www.sceptrebooks.co.uk

For my wife

A yellow bird
With a yellow bill
Was perched upon
My windowsill

I lured him in
With a piece of bread
And then I smashed
His fucking head…

— Traditional U.S. Army Marching Cadence

To be ignorant of evils to come, and forgetfull of evils past, is a mercifull provision in nature, whereby we digest the mixture of our few and evil dayes, and our delivered senses not relapsing into cutting remembrances, our sorrows are not kept raw by the edge of repetitions.

— Sir Thomas Browne

1

SEPTEMBER 2004

Al Tafar, Nineveh Province, Iraq

THE WAR TRIED to kill us in the spring. As grass greened the plains of Nineveh and the weather warmed, we patrolled the low-slung hills beyond the cities and towns. We moved over them and through the tall grass on faith, kneading paths into the windswept growth like pioneers. While we slept, the war rubbed its thousand ribs against the ground in prayer. When we pressed onward through exhaustion, its eyes were white and open in the dark. While we ate, the war fasted, fed by its own deprivation. It made love and gave birth and spread through fire.

Then, in summer, the war tried to kill us as the heat blanched all color from the plains. The sun pressed into our skin, and the war sent its citizens rustling into the shade of white buildings. It cast a white shade on everything, like a veil over our eyes. It tried to kill us every day, but it had not succeeded. Not that our safety was preordained. We were not destined to survive. The fact is, we were not destined at all. The war would take what it could get. It was patient. It didn't care about objectives, or boundaries, whether you were loved by many or not at all. While I slept that summer, the war came to me in my dreams and showed me its sole purpose: to go on, only to go on. And I knew the war would have its way.

The war had killed thousands by September. Their bodies lined the pocked avenues at irregular intervals. They were hidden in alleys, were found in bloating piles in the troughs of the hills outside the cities, the faces puffed and green, allergic now to life. The war had tried its best to kill us all: man, woman, child. But it had killed fewer than a thousand soldiers like me and Murph. Those numbers still meant something to us as what passed for fall began. Murph and I had agreed. We didn't want to be the thousandth killed. If we died later, then we died. But let that number be someone else's milestone.

We hardly noticed a change when September came. But I know now that everything that will ever matter in my life began then. Perhaps light came a little more slowly to the city of Al Tafar, falling the way it did beyond thin shapes of rooflines and angled promenades in the dark. It fell over buildings in the city, white and tan, made of clay bricks roofed with corrugated metal or concrete. The sky was vast and catacombed with clouds. A cool wind blew down from the distant hillsides we'd been patrolling all year. It passed over the minarets that rose above the citadel, flowed down through alleys with their flapping green awnings, out over the bare fields that ringed the city, and finally broke up against the scattered dwellings from which our rifles bristled. Our platoon moved around our rooftop position, gray streaks against the predawn light. It was still late summer then, a Sunday, I think. We waited.

For four days we had crawled along the rooftop grit. We slipped and slid on a carpeting of loose brass casings left over from the previous days' fighting. We curled ourselves into absurd shapes and huddled below the whitewashed walls of our position. We stayed awake on amphetamines and fear.

I pushed my chest off the rooftop and crested the low wall, trying to scan the few acres of the world for which we were responsible. The squat buildings beyond the field undulated through the tinny green of my scope. Bodies were scattered about from the past four days of fighting in the open space between our positions and the rest of Al Tafar. They lay in the dust, broken and shattered and bent, their white shifts gone dark with blood. A few smoldered among the junipers and spare tufts of grass, and there was a heady mix of carbon and bolt oil and their bodies burning in the newly crisp air of morning.

I turned around, ducked back below the wall and lit a cigarette, shielding the cherry in my curled palm. I pulled long drags off it and blew the smoke against the top of the roof, where it spread out, then rose and disappeared. The ash grew long and hung there and a very long time seemed to pass before it fell to the ground.

The rest of the platoon on the roof started to move and jostle with the flickering half-light of dawn. Sterling perched with his rifle over the wall, sleeping and starting throughout our waiting. He jerked his head back occasionally and swiveled to see if anyone had caught him. He showed me a broad disheveled grin in the receding dark, held up his trigger finger and daubed Tabasco sauce into his eyes to stay awake. He turned back toward our sector, and his muscles visibly bucked and tensed beneath his gear.

Murph's breath was a steady comfort to my right. I had grown accustomed to it, the way he'd punctuate its rhythm with a well-practiced spit into an acrid pool of dark liquid that always seemed to be growing between us. He smiled up at me. "Want a rub, Bart?" I nodded. He passed me a can of care-package Kodiak, and I jammed it into the cup of my bottom lip, snubbing out my cigarette. The wet tobacco bit and made my eyes water. I spat into the pool between us. I was awake. Out of the gray early morning the city became whole. White flags hung in a few scattered windows in the buildings beyond the bodies in the field. They formed an odd crochet where the window's dark recesses were framed by jagged glass. The windows themselves were set into whitewashed buildings that became ever brighter in the sun. A thin fog off the Tigris dissipated, revealing what hints of life remained, and in the soft breeze from the hills to the north the white rags of truce fluttered above those same green awnings.

Sterling tapped at the face of his watch. We knew the muezzin's song would soon warble its eerie fabric of minor notes out from the minarets, calling the faithful to prayer. It was a sign and we knew what it meant, that hours had passed, that we had drawn nearer to our purpose, which was as vague and foreign as the indistinguishable dawns and dusks with which it came.

"On your toes, guys!" the LT called in a forceful whisper.

Murph sat up and calmly worked a small dot of lubricant into the action of his rifle. He chambered a round and rested the barrel against the low wall. He stared off into the gray angles where the streets and alleys opened onto the field to our front. I could see into his blue eyes, the whites spider-webbed with red. They had fallen farther into his sockets during the past few months. There were times when I looked at him and could only see two small shadows, two empty holes. I let the bolt push a round into the chamber of my rifle and nodded at him. "Here we go again," I said. He smiled from the corner of his mouth. "Same old shit again," he answered.

We'd come to that building as the moon flagged to a sliver in the first hours of the battle. There were no lights on. We crashed our vehicle through a flimsy metal gate that had once been painted dark red but had since rusted over, so that it was hard to tell what part had been painted red and what part was rust. When the ramp dropped from our vehicle we rushed to the door. A few soldiers from first squad rushed to the back, and the rest of the platoon stacked up at the front. We kicked in both doors at the same time and ran in. The building was empty. As we went through each room, the lights affixed to the front of our rifles cut narrow cylinders through the dark interior, but they were not bright enough to see by. The lights showed the dust we'd kicked up. Chairs had been turned over in some of the rooms, and colorfully woven rugs hung over the windowsills where the glass had been shot out. There were no people. In some of the rooms we thought we saw people and we yelled out sharply for the people who were not there to get on the floor. We went through each room like that until we got to the roof. When we got to the roof, we looked out over the field. The field was flat and made of dust and the city was dark behind it.

At daybreak on the first day our interpreter, Malik, came out onto the flat concrete roof and sat next to me where I leaned against the wall. It was not yet light, but it almost appeared to be because the sky was white the way the sky is when heavy with snow. We heard fighting across the city, but it had not reached us yet. Only the noise of rockets and machine guns and helicopters swooping down near vertical in the distance told us we were in a war.

"This is my old neighborhood," he told me.

His English was exceptional. There was a glottal sound in his voice, but it was not harsh. I'd often asked him to help me with my sparse Arabic, trying to get my pronunciation of this or that word right. "Shukran." "Afwan." "Qumbula." *Thank you. You're welcome. Bomb.* He'd help, but he always ended our exchanges by saying, "My friend, I need to speak English. For the practice." He'd been a student at the university before the war, studying literature. When the university closed, he came to us. He wore a hood over his face, worn khaki slacks and a faded dress shirt that appeared to be ironed freshly every day. He never took his mask off. The one time Murph and I had asked him about it, he took his index finger and traced the fringe of the hood that hung around his neck. "They'll kill me for helping you. They'll kill my whole family."

Murph hunched low and trotted over from the other side of the roof where he had been helping the LT and Sterling set up the machine gun after we'd arrived. Watching him move, I got the impression that the flatness of the desert made him nervous. That somehow the low ridgelines in the distance made the dried brown grasses of the floodplain even more unbearable.

"Hey, Murph," I said. "This is Malik's old stomping grounds."

Murph ducked quickly and sat next to the wall. "Whereabouts?" he asked.

Malik stood up and pointed to a strip of buildings that seemed to grow organically in odd, not quite ninety-degree sections. The buildings stood beyond the field at the beginning of our sector. A little farther past the outskirts of Al Tafar, there was an orchard. Fires burned from steel drums and trash heaps and sprung up seemingly without cause around the edges of the city. Murph and I did not stand up, but we saw where Malik pointed.

"Mrs. Al-Sharifi used to plant her hyacinth in this field." He spread his hands out wide and moved his arms in a sweeping motion that reminded me of convocation.

Murph reached for the cuff of Malik's pressed shirt. "Careful, big guy. You're gonna get silhouetted."

"She was this crazy old widow." He had his hands on his hips. His eyes were glazed over with exhaustion. "The women in the neighborhood were so jealous of those flowers." Malik laughed. "They accused her of using magic to make them grow the way they did." He'd paused then, and put his hands on the dried mud wall we'd been leaning against. "They were burned up in the battle last fall. She did not try to replant them this year," he finished brusquely.

I tried to imagine living there but could not, even though we had patrolled the same streets Malik was talking about and drank tea in the small clay hovels and I'd had my hands wrapped in the thinly veined hands of the old men and women who lived in them. "All right, buddy," I said. "You're gonna get your ass shot off if you don't get down."

"It is a shame you didn't see those hyacinths," he said.

And then it started. It seemed as if the movement of one moment to the next had its own trajectory, a thing both finite and expansive, like the endless divisibility of numbers strung out on a line. The tracers reached out from all the dark spaces in the buildings across the field, and there were many more bullets than streaks of phosphorescence. We heard them tear at the air around our ears and smack into the clay brick and concrete. We did not see Malik get killed, but Murph and I had his blood on both of our uniforms. When we got the order to cease fire we looked over the low wall and he was lying in the dust and there was a lot of blood around him.

"Doesn't count, does it?" Murph asked.

"No. I don't think so."

"What're we at?"

"Nine sixty-eight? Nine seventy? We'll have to check the paper when we get back."

I was not surprised by the cruelty of my ambivalence then. Nothing seemed more natural than someone getting killed. And now, as I reflect on how I felt and behaved as a boy of twenty-one from my position of safety in a warm cabin above a clear stream in the Blue Ridge, I can only tell myself that it was necessary. I needed to continue. And to continue, I had to see the world with clear eyes, to focus on the essential. We only pay attention to rare things, and death was not rare.

Rare was the bullet with your name on it, the IED buried just for you. Those were the things we watched for.

I didn't think about Malik much after that. He was an incidental figure who only seemed to exist in his relation to my continuing life. I couldn't have articulated it then, but I'd been trained to think war was the great unifier, that it brought people closer together than any other activity on earth. Bullshit. War is the great maker of solipsists: how are you going to save my life today? Dying would be one way. If you die, it becomes more likely that I will not. You're nothing, that's the secret: a uniform in a sea of numbers, a number in a sea of dust. And we somehow thought those numbers were a sign of our own insignificance. We thought that if we remained ordinary, we would not die. We confused correlation with cause and saw a special significance in the portraits of the dead, arranged neatly next to the number corresponding to their place on the growing list of casualties we read in the newspapers, as indications of an ordered war. We had a sense, something we only felt in the brief flash of synapse to synapse, that these names had been on the list long before the dead had come to Iraq. That the names were there as soon as those portraits had been taken, a number given, a place assigned. And that they'd been dead from that moment forward. When we saw the name Sgt. Ezekiel Vasquez, twenty-one, Laredo, Texas, #748, killed by small-arms fire in Baqubah, Iraq, we were sure that he'd walked as a ghost for years through

South Texas. We thought he was already dead on the flight over, that if he was scared when the C-141 bringing him to Iraq had pitched and yawed through the sky above Baghdad there had been no need. He had nothing to fear. He'd been invincible, absolutely, until the day he was not. The same, too, for Spc. Miriam Jackson, nineteen, Trenton, New Jersey, #914, dead as a result of wounds sustained in a mortar attack in Samarra, at Landsthul Regional Medical Center. We were glad. Not that she was killed, only that we were not. We hoped that she'd been happy, that she took advantage of her special status before she inevitably arrived under that falling mortar, having gone out to hang her freshly washed uniform on a line behind her connex.

Of course, we were wrong. Our biggest error was thinking that it mattered what we thought. It seems absurd now that we saw each death as an affirmation of our lives. That each one of those deaths belonged to a time and that therefore that time was not ours. We didn't know the list was limitless. We didn't think beyond a thousand. We never considered that we could be among the walking dead as well. I used to think that maybe living under that contradiction had guided my actions and that one decision made or unmade in adherence to this philosophy could have put me on or kept me off the list of the dead.

I know it isn't like that now. There were no bullets with my name on them, or with Murph's, for that matter. There were no bombs made just for us. Any of them would have killed us just as well as they'd killed the owners of those names. We didn't have a time laid out for us, or a place. I have stopped wondering about those inches to the left and right of my head, the three-miles-an-hour difference that would have put us directly over an IED. It never happened. I didn't die. Murph did. And though I wasn't there when it happened, I believe unswervingly that when Murph was killed, the dirty knives that stabbed him were addressed "To whom it may concern." Nothing made us special. Not living. Not dying. Not even being ordinary. Still, I like to think there was a ghost of compassion in me then, and that if I'd had a chance to see those hyacinths I would have noticed them.

Malik's body, crumpled and broken at the foot of the building, didn't shock me. Murph passed me a smoke and we lay down beneath the wall again. But I could not stop thinking about a woman Malik's conversation had reminded me of, who'd served us tea in small, finely blemished cups. The memory seemed impossibly distant, buried in the dust, waiting for some brush to uncover it. I remembered how she'd blushed and smiled, and how impossible it was for her to not be beautiful, despite her age, a paunch, a few teeth gone brown and her skin appearing like the cracked, dry clay of summer.

Perhaps that is how it was: a field full of hyacinth. It was not like that when we stormed the building, not like that four days after Malik died. The green grasses that waved in the breeze were burned by fire and the summer sun. The festival of people on the market street with their long white shifts and loud voices were gone. Some of them were lying dead in the courtyards of the city or in its lace of alleys. The rest walked or rode in sluggish caravans, on foot or in orange and white jalopies, in mule-drawn carts or in huddled groups of twos and threes, women and men, the old and young, the whole and wounded. All that was the life of Al Tafar left in a drab parade out of the city. They walked past our gates, past Jersey walls and gun emplacements, out into the dry September hills. They did not raise their eyes in the curfewed hours. They were a speckled line of color in the dark and they were leaving.

A radio crackled in the rooms beneath us. The lieutenant quietly gave our situation report to our command. "Yes, sir," he said, "roger, sir," and it passed, at each level more removed from us, until I am sure somewhere someone was told, in a room that was warm and dry and safe, that eighteen soldiers had watched the alleys and streets of Al Tafar through the night and that X number of enemies were lying dead in a dusty field.

The day had almost broken over the city and the ridges in the desert when the low, electric noise of the radio was replaced by the sound of the lieutenant's boots padding up the staircase to the roof. Mere outlines took shape, and the city, vague and notional at night, became a contoured and substantial thing before us. I looked west. Tans and greens emerged in the light. The gray of mud walls, of buildings and courtyards arranged in squat honeycombs, receded with the rising sun. A few fires burned in the grove of thin and ordered fruit trees a little to the south. The smoke rose through a gently tattered canopy of leaves only slightly taller than a man and leaned obediently to the wind coming across the valley.

The lieutenant came up to the roof and lowered himself into a slouch, his upper body parallel to the earth, his legs chugging, until he reached the wall. He sat with his back against the wall and gestured for us to gather around him.

"All right, guys. This is the deal."

Murph and I leaned against each other until the weight of our bodies found their balance. Sterling inched closer to the lieutenant and fixed his eyes in a hard glare that traversed the rest of us on the roof. I looked at the lieutenant as he spoke. His eyes were dim. Before he continued he let out a short, bright sigh and rubbed a rash the color of washed-out raspberries with two fingers. It covered a small oval from his sharp brow line down onto his left cheek and seemed to follow the rounded path of his eye socket.

The LT was a distant person by nature. I don't even remember where he was from. There was something restrained about him, something more than simple adherence to nonfraternization. It was not elitism. He seemed to be unknowable, or slightly adrift. He sighed often. "We're here until midday or so," he said. "Third platoon is going to push through the alleys to our northwest and try to flush them to our front. Hopefully they'll be too scared to do much shooting at us before we..." He paused and brought his hand down from his face, reached into the pockets on his chest beneath his body armor and fished for a cigarette. I handed him one. "Thanks, Bartle," he said. He turned to look at the orchard burning to the south. "How long have those fires been going?"

"Probably started last night," said Murph.

"OK, you and Bartle keep an eye on that."

The column of smoke that bent beneath the wind had straightened. It cut a black runny line across the sky.

"What was I saying before that?" The lieutenant looked absently over his shoulder and inched his eyes up over the wall. "Fuck me," he muttered.

A specialist from second squad said, "Hey, no sweat, LT, we got it."

Sterling cut him off. "Shut the fuck up. LT's done when he says he's fucking done."

I didn't realize it then, but Sterling seemed to know exactly how hard to push the LT so that discipline remained. He didn't care if we hated him. He knew what was necessary. He smiled at me and his straight, white teeth reflected the early morning sun. "You were saying, sir, that hopefully they'll be too scared to shoot before..." The LT opened his mouth to finish his thought, but Sterling continued, "Before we fucking kill the hajji fucks."

The lieutenant nodded his head and slouched over and trotted downstairs. We crawled back to our positions to wait. A fire had begun to burn in the town, its source obscured by walls and alleys. Thick black smoke seemed to join from a hundred fires all over Al Tafar, becoming one long curl up toward heaven.

The sun gathered itself behind us, rising in the east, warming the collar of my blouse, baking in the salt that clotted in hard lines and snaked around our necks and arms. I turned my head and looked right into it. I had to close my eyes, but I could still see its shape, a white hole in the darkness, before I turned west again and opened them.

Two minarets rose, like arms, up from the dusty buildings, slightly obscured now and then by smoke. They were dormant. No sound had come from them that morning. No adhan had been called. The long line of refugees that snaked its way out of the city for the past four days had slowed. Only a few old men bent over worn canes of cedar shuffled between the field of dead and the grove of trees. Two gaunt dogs bounced around them, nipped their heels, retreated when struck, and then started in on them again.

And it began once more. The orchestral whine of falling mortars arrived from all around us. Even after so many months beneath them, there was a blank confusion on the faces of the platoon. We stared at one another with mouths agape, fingers strangling the grips of our rifles. It was a clear dawn in September in Al Tafar, and the war seemed narrowly focused, as if it occurred only in this place, and I remember feeling like I had jumped into a cold river on the first warm day of spring, wet and scared and breathing hard, with nothing to do but swim.

"Incoming!"

We moved by rote, our bodies made prostrate, our fingers interlaced behind our heads, our mouths open to keep the pressure balanced.

And then the sound of the impacts echoed off into the morning. I didn't raise my head until the last reverberation faded.

I looked over the wall slowly, and a din of voices shouted, "All clear!" and "I'm up!"

"Bartle?" Murph huffed.

"I'm up, I'm up," I said quietly, and I was breathing very hard and I looked out over the field and there were wounds in the earth and in the already dead and battered bodies and a few small juniper trees were turned up and on their sides where the mortars fell. Sterling ran to the opening in the floor and yelled down to the LT, "Up, sir." He moved to each one of us on the roof, smacking the back of our helmets. "Get ready, motherfuckers," he said.

I hated him. I hated the way he excelled in death and brutality and domination. But more than that, I hated the way he was necessary, how I needed him to jar me into action even when they were trying to kill me, how I felt like a coward until he screamed into my ear, "Shoot these hajji fucks!"

I hated the way I loved him when I inched up out of the terror and returned fire, seeing him shooting too, smiling the whole time, screaming, the whole rage and hate of these few acres, alive and spreading, in and through him.

And they did come, shadowed in windows. They came out from behind woven prayer rugs and fired off bursts and the bullets whipped past and we'd duck and listen as they smacked against the concrete and mud-brick and little pieces flew in every direction. They ran through trash-strewn alleys, past burning drums and plastic blowing like clumps of thistle over the ancient cobblestones.

Sterling yelled a long time that day before I squeezed the trigger. My ears had already rung out from the noise and the first bullet I released into the field seemed to leave my rifle with a dull pop. It kicked up a little cloud of dust when it hit and it was surrounded by many other little clouds of dust just like it.

Rounds by the hundreds shook dust off the ground, the trees and buildings. An old car crumpled and collapsed beneath the dust. Once in a while, someone ran between the buildings, behind the orange and white cars, over the rooftops, and they'd surround themselves with little clouds of dust.

A man ran behind a low wall in a courtyard and looked around, astonished to be alive, his weapon cradled in his arms. My first instinct was to yell out to him, "You made it, buddy, keep going," but I remembered how odd it would be to say a thing like that. It was not long before the others saw him too.

He looked left, then right, and the dust popped around him, and I wanted to tell everyone to stop shooting at him, to ask, "What kind of men are we?" An odd sensation came over me, as if I had been saved, for I was not a man, but a boy, and that he may have been frightened, but I didn't mind that so much, because I was frightened too, and I realized with a great shock that I was shooting at him and that I wouldn't stop until I was sure that he was dead, and I felt better knowing we were killing him together and that it was just as well not to be sure you are the one who did it.

But I knew. I shot him and he slumped over behind the wall. He was shot again by someone else and the bullet went through his chest and ricocheted, breaking a potted plant hanging from a window above the courtyard. Then he was shot again and he fell at a strange angle — backward over his bent legs — and most of the side of his face was gone and there was a lot of blood and it pooled around him in the dust.

A car drove toward us along the road between the orchard and the field of dead. Two large white sheets billowed from its rear windows. Sterling ran to the other side of the building, where the machine gun was set up. I looked through my scope and saw an old man behind the wheel and an elderly woman in the back passenger seat.

Sterling laughed. "Come on, motherfuckers."

He couldn't see them. I'll yell, I thought. I'll tell him they are old, let them pass.

But bullets bit at the crumbling road around the car. They punched into the sheet metal.

I said nothing. I followed the car with my scope. The old woman ran her fingers along a string of pale beads. Her eyes were closed.

I couldn't breathe.

The car stopped in the middle of the road, but Sterling did not stop the shooting. The bullets ripped through the car and out the other side. The holes in the car funneled light, and the smoke and dust hung in the light. The door opened and she fell from the old car. She tried to drag herself to the side of the road. She crawled. Her old blood mixed with the ash and dust. She stopped moving.

"Holy shit, that bitch got murdered," Murph said. There was no grief, or anguish, or joy, or pity in that statement. There was no judgment made. He was just surprised, like he was waking from a long afternoon nap, disoriented, realizing that the world has continued uninterrupted in spite of the strange things that may have happened while you slept. He could have said that it was Sunday, as we did not know what day it was. And it would have been a sudden thing to notice that it was Sunday at a time like that. But he spoke the truth either way, and it wouldn't have mattered much if it had been Sunday, and since none of us

22

had slept in a long time, none of it really seemed to matter much at all.

Sterling sat down behind the wall next to the machine gun. He waved us to him and took a piece of pound cake from the cargo pocket on his trousers as we listened to the final bursts of nervous firing peter out. He broke the dry cake into three pieces. "Take this," he said. "Eat."

The smoke rose and began to disappear. I watched the old woman bleed on the side of the road. The dust blew in languid waves and began to swirl slightly. We heard shots again. Beyond a building a small girl with auburn curls and a tattered sundress stepped out toward the old woman. Errant bullets from other positions kicked up the dust around her in dry blooms.

We looked to Sterling. He waved us off. "Someone get on the net and tell those fuckers it's a just a kid," he said.

The girl ducked behind the building, then emerged again, this time shuffling toward the old woman very slowly. She tried dragging the body, and her face contorted with effort as she pulled the old woman by her one complete arm. The girl described circles into the fine dust as she paced around the body. The path they made was marked in blood: from the car smoking and ablaze, through a courtyard ringed by hyacinths, to the place where the woman lay dead, attended by the small child, who rocked and moved her lips, perhaps singing some desert elegy that I couldn't hear.

The ash from the burning of clay bricks and the fat of

lean men and women covered everything. The pale minarets dominated the smoke, and the sky was still pale like snow. The city seemed to reach upward out of the settling dust. Our part was over, for a while at least. It was September and though there were few trees from which leaves could fall, some did. They shook off the scarred and slender branches, buffeted by the wind and light descending from the hills to the north. I tried to count the leaves as they fell, removed from their moorings by the impact of mortars and bombs. They shook. A thin sheaf of dust floated off each one.

I looked at Murph and Sterling and the rest of the platoon on the roof. The LT walked to each of us and put his hand on our arms, speaking softly, trying to soothe us with the sound of his voice, the way one would with frightened horses. Perhaps our eyes were wet and black, perhaps we bared our teeth. "Good job," and "You're OK," and "We're gonna be OK," he said. It was hard to believe that we'd be OK and that we'd fought well. But I remember being told that the truth does not depend on being believed.

The radio came on again. Before long the LT would give us another mission. We would be tired when the mission came, but we would go, for we had no alternative. Perhaps we'd had them once: alternatives, other paths to take. But our course was certain then, if unknown. It was going to be dark before we knew it. We had lived, Murph and me.

I try so hard now to remember if I saw any hint of what was coming, if there was some shadow over him, some way

I could have known he was so close to being killed. In my memory of those days on the rooftop, he is half a ghost. But I didn't see it then, and couldn't. No one can see that. I guess I'm glad I didn't know, because we were happy that morning in Al Tafar, in September. Our relief was coming. The day was full of light and warm. We slept.

2

DECEMBER 2003

Fort Dix, New Jersey

MRS. LADONNA MURPHY, rural mail carrier, would have only needed to read the first word of the letter to know that it had not been written by her son. The truth is, she had not received all that many letters from him, so when I wrote it, I took a guess that she might not have that much to compare it to. He'd rarely been more than a few miles away from her during the first seventeen years of his life. About five miles, depending on where Daniel was, when she reached the farthest stop on her mail route if measured as the crow flies. Seven, if we allow for depth, at midnight, during those three months he worked in the Shipp Mountain Mine after he graduated from the Bluefield Vocational and Technical School. Then on to Benning in the fall, the farthest he'd ever been from home, where Daniel would write her a few short notes before lights-out, scrawling out his thoughts about the redness of the clay, the pleasure he took in sleeping under those endless Georgia stars and, when time allowed, making space for the assurances that boys like me and Daniel always end up sending to our families, assurances that were as much for us as for them. The rest of his life he'd spent with me. Ten months, give or take, from the time he appeared next to me in formation that day in New Jersey with the snow so high over our boots that our left and right faces made only a whisper in the snow. Ten months, give or take, from that day to the day he died. It might seem like a short time, but my whole life since has merely been a digression from those days, which now hang over me like a quarrel that will never be resolved.

I'd had this idea once that you had to grow old before you died. I still feel like there is some truth to it, because Daniel Murphy had grown old in the ten months I'd known him. And perhaps it was a need for something to make sense that caused me to pick up a pencil and write a letter to a dead boy's mother, to write it in his name, having known him plenty long enough to know it was not his way to call his mother "Mom." I'd known a lot, really. I'd known that snow comes early in the year in the mountains where Daniel was from, November, sure, and sometimes as early as October. But I only found out later that she'd read that letter with snow falling all around her. That she'd set it on the seat next to her while she mushed her old right-hand-drive Jeep up and down the switchbacks on her route, carving clean tracks through the white erasure that had fallen all throughout the night before. And that as she pulled down the long gravel path leading to their little house, on the winter-dormant apple orchard Daniel had talked about so often, she kept sneaking glances at the return address. She must have taken those glances with an unusual level of skepticism for a rural mail carrier as experienced as she was, because she thought each time that something different would be written there. When the wheels of her old Jeep finally stopped, and the whole mass of '84 metal slid a few last feet in the snow, she'd taken the letter in both hands and become briefly, terrifyingly happy.

At one time you could have asked me if I thought the snow meant something and I would have said yes. I might have thought there was some significance to the fact that there had been snow on the day Murph had come into my life and snow on the day I willed myself into the one that had been taken from him. I may not have believed it, but I'm sure I would have wanted to. It's lovely to think that snow can be special. We're always told it is. Of all those million million flakes that fall, no two are alike, forever and ever, amen. I've spent some time looking out the window of my cabin watching snowflakes fall like a shot dove's feathers fluttering slowly down to the ground. They all look the same to me.

I know it was a terrible thing to write that letter. What I don't know is where it fits in with all of the other terrible things I think about. At some point along the way I stopped believing in significance. Order became an accident of observation. I've come to accept that parts of life are constant, that just because something happens on two different days doesn't make it a goddamn miracle. All I really know for sure is that no matter how long I live, and no matter how I spend that time, those scales aren't ever coming level. Murph's always going to be eighteen, and he's always going to be dead. And I'll be living with a promise that I couldn't keep.

I never intended to make the promise that I made. But something happened the day Murph pivoted and moved through the open rank of our formation, took his place in the squad next to me and looked up. He smiled. And the sun careened off the small drifts of snow, and he closed his eyes slightly against it, and they were blue. Now, so many years distant, I picture him turning to speak, with his arms clasped behind him at parade rest, and it seems like whatever he says back there in my memory could be the most important words I'll ever hear. In truth, he didn't seem special then. All he said was "Hi." He only came up to my shoulder in height, so when Sergeant Sterling, our newly assigned team leader, heard the muffled whisper Murph had made, he didn't see him. Instead, he saw me. He glared and clenched his teeth and barked, "At ease the fucking noise, Bartle." There is nothing else to be said. Something happened. I met Murph. The formation broke. It was cold in the shadow of the barracks.

"Bartle. Murphy. Get your stupid asses over here," called Sergeant Sterling.

Sterling had been assigned to our company when our deployment orders came through. He had been to Iraq already, on the first push north out of Kuwait, and had been decorated, so even the higher-ups looked at him with admiration. And it wasn't just the fact of his having been there that caused us to respect him. He was harsh, but fair, and there was a kind of evolutionary beauty in his competence. His carriage seemed different only by a matter of degree from the way our other sergeants and officers acted. I noticed the way his whole upper body moved in concert with his rifle on field exercises, pivoting against the backdrop of the snow in the branches of the hardwoods, his legs propelling him purposefully forward, where he'd stop in a clearing and kneel. The way he'd remove his helmet slowly, showing his cropped blond hair, his blue eyes scanning the brush at the wood line. And he'd listen and I'd watch and we'd wait, the whole platoon, for him to make some determination. We would trust him when he pointed and told us to move on. It was easy to follow him wherever he was going.

Murph and I walked to Sterling and stood at parade rest. "All right, little man," he said, "I want you to get in Bartle's back pocket and I want you to stay there. Do you understand?"

Murph looked at me before he answered. I tried to make a face that would clearly communicate the need for his answer to come quickly, and for it to be directed toward Sergeant Sterling. But he didn't answer, and Sterling smacked him on the side of the head, knocking his cover to the ground, where little drifts of snow sketched the December wind.

"Roger, Sergeant," I said. I pulled Murph toward the awning of the barracks door, where a cluster of guys from second platoon were smoking. As we walked, Sterling called behind us, "You guys seriously need to unfuck yourselves. None of you people get it."

We turned to look at him when we got to the door. He had his hands on his hips, and his head was tilted skyward. His eyes were closed. It was getting dark, but he didn't move. He waited, as if waiting for whichever last shadow would cause evening.

Murph and I got up to our eight-man room on the third floor of the battalion barracks and I closed the door. Everyone else was milling around base on an evening pass. We were alone. "You got your bunk and locker?" I asked.

"Yeah," he said. "It's down the hall."

"Swap your shit out and get a rack near me."

He left the room with a shuffle. As I waited for him I thought about what I would tell him. I'd been in the army a couple of years. It had been good to me, more or less, a place to disappear. I kept my head down and did as I was told. Nobody expected much of me, and I hadn't asked for much in return. I hadn't given a lot of thought to actually going to war, but it was happening now, and I was still struggling to find a sense of urgency that seemed proportional to the events unfolding in my life. I remember feeling relief in basic while everyone else was frantic with fear. It had dawned on me that I'd never have to make a decision again. That seemed freeing, but it gnawed at some part of me even then. Eventually, I had to learn that freedom is not the same thing as the absence of accountability.

Murph came back into the room with a kind of waddle under the weight of his gear. He looked a lot like Sterling in some ways, the blond hair and blue eyes. But it was as if Murph was the ordinary version. Where Sterling was tall and trimly muscled, Murph was not. He wasn't fat, it was just that he seemed almost incorrectly short and squat by comparison. Whereas Sterling's jawline could have been transferred directly from a geometry textbook, Murph's features were nearly imperceptibly askew. Whereas Murph's mouth fell comfortably into a smile, Sterling's did not. Maybe all I noticed was a condition of reality, applicable everywhere on earth: some people are extraordinary and some are not. Sterling was, though I could see at times that he bristled at the consequences of this condition. When he first came to our company, the captain introduced him to us by saying, "Sergeant Sterling will be put on the fucking recruiting posters, men. Mark my words." When the formation broke, I walked past them and overheard Sterling say, "I will never ask anyone to do this, sir. Never." And I noticed as he walked away that he wasn't wearing any of the awards on his Class A's that the captain had rattled off with such poorly hidden envy. But wars need ordinary boys, too.

After we put his gear in his locker I sat down on a bottom bunk and Murph sat on the one across from me. The room was bright from the sheen of fluorescent paneling above us. The shadeless windows looked out onto night and snow, circles of lamplight and the red brick of other barracks. "Where are you from?" I asked.

"Southwest Virginia," he said. "What about you?"

"A little shithole town outside Richmond."

He looked disappointed by my answer. "Hell," he said, "I didn't know you was from Virginia."

Something about that fact irritated me. "Yeah," I said smugly. "We're practically related." I regretted saying it immediately. But I didn't want to be responsible for him. I didn't even want to be responsible for myself, but that wasn't his fault. I began to lay out my gear. "What'd you do down there in the sticks, Murph?" I took a wire brush to all the metallic components of my equipment, the small buttons and the hooks for straps, cleaning off the tarnish and oxidation of lying in the snow while preparing to fight in the desert. As Murph began to answer, the thought crossed my mind that something can only be absurd if enough people take it very seriously. When I looked back over at him, he had started to list facts about himself on the fingers of his small right hand. He hadn't yet moved to his index finger before pausing. "Yeah, I guess that's about it. Not much."

I hadn't even been listening. I could tell he was embarrassed. He hung his head a little and grabbed his gear from the locker and began to mirror my actions. For a while we were alone. The sound of the wire brushes roughing against green nylon and little pieces of metal settled into the room with a low hum. I understood. Being from a place where a few facts are enough to define you, where a few habits can fill a life, causes a unique kind of shame. We'd had small lives, populated by a longing for something more substantial than dirt roads and small dreams. So we'd come here, where life needed no elaboration and others would tell us who to be. When we finished our work we went to sleep, calm and free of regret.

Days passed. We came closer to our ship-out date, which was still being kept a secret by the higher-ups. But we felt it looming. The war had become a presence in our lives. We were grooms before a marriage. We trained in the snowy fields. We left the barracks in the morning, went to classrooms for briefings on the social structures and demographics of the unnamed towns that we'd be fighting for. We'd leave the classrooms at night with the sun already fallen as if by accident, somewhere to the west beyond the base's barbwire fencing.

The last week we were in New Jersey, Sterling came to see us in our room. We were packing up all of our gear that we knew we wouldn't need. The higher-ups had told us we'd have a pass soon and that our families would be able to see us for a last visit before our battalion's movement. The only thing left was a final range day, put in place as the result of a suggestion Sergeant Sterling had passed up the chain of command. When Sterling stepped through our door, he waved off our somewhat lazy effort to rise to parade rest.

"Sit down, guys," he said.

Murph and I sat down on my bunk, and Sterling sat down on the bunk across from us, rubbing his temples.

"How old are you two?"

"Eighteen," Murph answered quickly. "My birthday was last week," he said, smiling.

I was surprised he hadn't told me and a little surprised by how young he was. I was twenty-one then, and eighteen had never seemed so young until I heard the number said out loud. I looked at Murph sitting next to me on the bunk. He had a pimple on his chin, but otherwise his skin was smooth. It dawned on me that he'd never even shaved. The soft down on his cheekbones beneath his ears glowed whitely under the panel lights. I heard myself say, "Twenty-one." And now, as I remember it, I can feel how young I was. I can feel my body before it was scarred. I can reach to my cheek and for a moment remember how the skin was unblemished, then torn, and then healed below my eye like a wadi in miniature. "Twenty-one," I'd said, and I was as full of time as my body would allow. But looking back from where I am, almost thirty, old enough, I can see myself for what I was. Barely a man. Not a man. Life was in me, but it splashed as if at the bottom of a nearly empty bowl.

And so we looked at Sterling, distraught, and he said, "Fuck," and I knew that when he told us his age it would not be much more than ours. "All right, look," he said. "You guys are my guys."

"Roger, Sarge," we said.

"Our AO just came down from higher. It's gonna be a goat fuck. You guys have to promise to do what I say."

"OK. Sure thing, Sarge."

"Don't give me that shit, Privates. No 'sure thing' this time. Tell me you'll do what I say. Every. Fucking. Time." He beat the notes with his fist into the palm of his left hand.

"We'll do what you say. We promise," I said.

He took a deep breath and smiled. His shoulders sagged slightly.

"So, where is it, Sarge?" Murph asked.

"Al Tafar. Up north, near Syria. Like a hajji proving ground up there. Gets real fucking heated sometimes. I wasn't supposed to tell you yet, but I need you to understand something." He was slouched beneath the bunk above him. It caused him to lean slightly forward toward us and across the white space of the buffed tile floor.

Murph and I looked at each other and waited for him to continue.

"People are going to die," he said flatly. "It's statistics." Then he got up and left the room.

Somehow I slept, but fitfully. I'd wake from time to time and look out to see how the frost had gathered on the windowpanes. Murph called to me once, in the small hours before daybreak, and asked me if I thought we'd be OK. I kept looking out the window, even though the night had covered it over completely with a small layering of ice. A streetlamp glowed with a pale orange through the opacity. The air was cool and crisp in the room and I pulled my rough wool blanket tight around me. "Yeah, Murph. We'll be OK," I said. But I didn't believe it.

In the morning, before first light, we dragged ourselves over the sides of the company's deuce-and-a-half trucks and convoyed to the range. The snow had changed to rain overnight and we pulled our hoods over our helmets as far as we could. The rain was cold, percussive. The drops slid down the backs of our blouses and jackets, each one seemingly on the cusp of freezing. No one talked.

When we got to the range, we circled in the grayish snow for our safety briefing. I was tired and had a hard time focusing. The voices of the range cadre barked out through the mist like an unpracticed choir. I watched the rain fall onto the dead leaves, causing a kind of shimmer in the nearly naked branches. The sound of magazines being loaded by the range detail carried over the thin winter air from the dilapidated ammo shed. The white paint peeling off the sides reminded me of a country church I'd passed on my way to school as a boy. The noise emanating from the shed was strange and mechanical and droned in my ears until I couldn't hear a word the safety officers said. Sterling and Murph had taken their places in line to be rodded onto the range. Sterling glared at me, then cupped his rifle into the crook of his elbow and pointed at his watch. "Waiting on you, Private," he said.

Sterling was attentive in his marksmanship instruction. Murph and I both had our highest qualification scores ever. Sterling was pleased with us and seemed to be in a good mood. "Anything less than forty out of forty is operator error," he said. We moved to a small hill that sloped down from the firing line. We relaxed and sat at his feet as he reclined on the hill, oblivious to the snow. "I think y'all might be all right." For a while we didn't speak. It was enough to be satisfied with his approval. The sun was still high over the berm at the end of the range when Murph started talking.

"What's it like over there, Sarge?" Murph asked sheepishly. He was sitting cross-legged in the snow, his rifle over his lap like he was cradling a doll.

Sterling laughed. "God, that fucking question." He had begun gathering rocks and tossing them into my upturned Kevlar.

Murph looked away from him.

He spoke firmly. "They aren't gonna pop up and wait for you to shoot them. Remember your fundamentals and you'll be able to do what needs to be done. It's hard at first, but it's simple. Anybody can do it. Get a steady position and a good sight picture, control your breathing and squeeze. For some people, it's tough after. But most people want to do it when the time comes."

"Hard to imagine," I said. "You know, whether we'll be one or the other?"

He paused. "Better get to fucking imagining." He started to chuckle again. "Just gotta dig deep. Find that nasty streak."

I listened to the crack of rifles on the line. Saw branches lift and shake off snow when birds took flight, startled at the sound. The sun was small and bright in the sky. The rain had let up to a noisy drizzle.

"How do we do that?" I asked.

Sterling feigned frustration, but I could tell our solid performance on the range had given us some latitude. "Don't worry. I'll help." He seemed to catch something spilling out of himself and corrected his bearing. My Kevlar was full of rocks.

"Shit," said Murph.

"We just gotta train it up. Practice, practice, practice," Sterling said. He laid his head down on the ground and put his feet on my upturned helmet.

Murph started to say something, but I put my hand on his shoulder. "Yeah, we get it, Sarge," I said.

He stood up and stretched. The whole back of his uniform was wet, but it didn't seem to bother him. "It was their idea," he said. "Don't forget that. It's their idea every time. They ought to kill themselves instead of us."

I wasn't sure who "they" were.

Murph was looking at the ground. "So...so what are we doing?"

"Don't worry so much, ladies. You two just hold the tail. Everything'll be cool."

"The tail?" I asked.

"Yeah," he responded. "Let me fuck the dog."

The reports of rifles disappeared. Our last task was over. We loaded back on the trucks, anxious for a pass and time with our families. I thought about what Sterling had said. I wasn't sure he wasn't crazy, but I trusted that he was brave. And I now know the extent of Sterling's bravery. It was narrowly focused, but it was pure and unadulterated. It was a kind of elemental self-sacrifice, free of ideology, free of logic. He would put himself on the gallows in another boy's place for no other reason than that he thought the noose was better suited to his neck.

And then we celebrated. There were banners and folding tables in the base gymnasium. Our families watched as we stood in formation while the battalion commander gave a rousing, earnest speech about duty, and the chaplain injected humor into somber tales of Our Lord and Savior Jesus Christ. And there were hamburgers and French fries and we were glad.

I brought a plate to my mother and sat across from her, a small distance away from the throngs of mothers hanging on their sons' shoulders, the fathers holding their hands on their hips, smiling on cue. She'd been crying. She rarely wore makeup but it ran down into the hollows of her eyes that day. It smudged on the back of her wrist where she'd rubbed the tears away while sitting in the barracks parking lot in our ancient gold Chrysler.

"I told you not to do this, John," she said.

I clenched my jaw. I was still young enough then for the weak mannerisms of rebellion. I had practiced them from the time I turned twelve until I left our house, when I got fed up with nothing and called the only cab that had ever graced our long gravel driveway. "It's done, Ma."

She paused and took a deep in-breath. "OK. I know," she said. "I'm sorry. Let's have a nice time." She smiled and patted the back of my hands where they sat on the table and her eyes welled a little.

And we did have a nice time. I was relieved. As I sat up listlessly the night before the range, I'd run through all the possibilities that lay before me. I became certain that I'd die, then certain that I'd live, then certain that I'd be wounded, then uncertain of anything. It had been all I could do to keep from pacing the cold tiles, looking out the window for some sign in the snow or the lamplight. I remained uncertain. But I settled on the fear that I would die and my mother would have to bury a son she thought was angry. That she'd take the flag and see me lowered into the brown Virginia dirt. That she'd hear the salute of rifle shots roll in quick succession through the air, the whole time thinking that they sounded like the door I slammed when I was eighteen and she was in the backyard picking honeysuckle off the fence.

I went outside to smoke and see my mother off. I kissed her on the cheek and surprised myself with the force of my lips. "You need to quit those things," she said.

"I know, Ma. I will." I stubbed the cherry out beneath my boot. She hugged me and I could smell her hair, her perfume, my whole life back home. "I'll write as soon as I can, OK?"

She stepped slowly away from me, raised her hand to wave and turned and walked toward the car. I remember following her taillights as they turned out of the parking lot, watched them grow smaller as they passed the PT field and turned again toward the guard shack at the base's exit, where they disappeared. I lit another cigarette.

Most of the families had gone by then. Most but Murph's mother and a few others I didn't know. I saw Murph leading her by the hand throughout the gymnasium, investigating each small cluster of remaining people briefly, then moving on. I didn't realize they were looking for me until Murph turned in my direction and I saw him mouth something to his mother. I got up from the chair where I'd been sitting and waited for them to cross over the painted lines of the basketball court that had been used for our festivities.

Mrs. LaDonna Murphy hugged me tightly when I met her. She was small and frail-looking in a weathered sort of way, but younger than my mother. She smiled broadly when she looked at me, still wrapping her arms around my waist, looking up and showing me teeth slightly browned by smoke. Her hair was a faded blond worn in a bun, and she had on jeans and a blue button-up work shirt.

"Five more minutes, men," one of the NCOs called.

She released me from her embrace and said excitedly, "I'm just so proud of you guys. Daniel's told me so much about you. I feel like I know you already."

"Yes, ma'am. Me too."

"So y'all are getting to be good friends?"

I looked over at Murph and he gave me an apologetic shrug. "Yes, ma'am," I said. "We room together and everything."

"Well, I want you to know if y'all need anything, I'm gonna take care of you. Y'all will get more care packages than anyone."

"That's really kind of you, Mrs. Murphy."

Sterling called Murph to help another private sweep up red, white and blue confetti from around the three-point line of the court.

"And you're gonna look out for him, right?" she asked.

"Um, yes, ma'am."

"And Daniel, he's doing a good job?"

"Yes, ma'am, very good." How the hell should I know, lady? I wanted to say. I barely knew the guy. Stop. Stop asking me questions. I don't want to be accountable. I don't know anything about this.

"John, promise me that you'll take care of him."

"Of course." Sure, sure, I thought. Now you reassure me and I'll go back and go to bed.

"Nothing's gonna happen to him, right? Promise that you'll bring him home to me."

"I promise," I said. "I promise I'll bring him home to you."

Sterling caught me later as I was walking back from the gym to our barracks. He was sitting on the front stoop and I stopped to smoke a cigarette. "It's kind of nice out tonight, huh, Sarge?"

He stood up and started pacing back and forth. "I overheard you talking to Private Murphy's mother."

"Oh, right. That."

"You shouldn't have done that, Private."

"What?"

He stopped and put his hands on his hips. "C'mon. Promises? Really? You're making fucking promises now?"

I was annoyed. "I was just trying to make her feel better, Sarge," I said. "It's not a big deal."

He knocked me to the ground quickly and hit me twice in the face, once below the eye and once directly in the mouth. I felt his knuckles fold my lips under my teeth. I felt my front teeth cut into my top lip, the blood running hot and metallic into my mouth. My lips swelled immediately. My cheek had been cut by a ring he wore on his right hand, and that blood gathered into runnels and ran down my face and into the corner of my eye and onto the snow. He stood over me with his feet on either side of my body, just looking at me. He shook the sting out of his hand in the cold air. "Report me if you want. I don't even fucking care anymore."

I lay in the snow for a while longer, picking out the constellations bright enough not to be obscured by the artificial light pouring out from the barracks windows and the street-lamps lining the nearby avenue. Saw Orion, saw Canis Major. When the lights went out in the barracks, I saw other stars, arranged as they had been a million years ago or more. I wondered what they looked like now. I got up and dragged myself up the stairs and into our room. Murph sat up, but the lights stayed off. I took off my uniform and threw it in my locker, then slid under the tight folds of the sheets.

"Tonight was good," he said. I didn't answer. I heard him turn in his bunk. "You OK?"

"Yeah, I'm good." I looked out the window, through the tops of the evergreen trees arranged in rows between the barracks. I knew that at least a few of the stars I saw were probably gone already, collapsed into nothing. I felt like I was looking at a lie. But I didn't mind. The world makes liars of us all.

3

MARCH 2005

Kaiserslautern, Rhineland-Palatinate, Germany

IT WASN'T LONG after I left Al Tafar that I began to feel very strange. I first noticed it on the highway between the air base and the town of Kaiserslautern. The trees outside the window of the taxi made a silver blur, but I could clearly see the green buds of spring as they untethered themselves from the remains of winter. It reminded me of the war, though I was only a week removed from it, and unbeknownst to me at the time, my memories would seem closer the farther I got from the circumstances that gave birth to them. I suppose, now, that they grew the same way other things grow. In the quiet of the taxi, the thin trees made me think of the war and how in the desert our year seemed like a seasonless thing, except in fall. There was a sharp disquiet in the way days passed into other days and the dust covered everything in Al Tafar, so that even the blooming hyacinth flowers became a kind of rumor.

I imagined it would be easier then, to arrive in a temperate place so obviously passing from winter into spring, but it was not. The wet, cold air of March in Germany shocked my skin, and when the LT said we wouldn't get a pass even though we couldn't leave until the next day, just wait it out, I decided I'd earned one anyway.

I'd had to walk a half a mile or so to get out the security gate and another two until the first row of buildings appeared on my left. The sky was now less brightly lit, and there was a steady, fine mist that hovered in the air. In the plane, the sun had a kind of buoyant dominance, but it had hidden itself away beyond clouds that appeared like pale, soot-colored sketches of themselves. The buildings were more colorful than I thought buildings could be, with light pastel trims, and rich creams and yellows thickly painted on the stucco walls. I walked toward the town, past softly lit cafes emitting deep, hearthy smells, past solitary people walking on the street, the collars of their slickers pulled tightly around their necks, their eyes pausing to evaluate me. Without fail, they turned toward some other ending for their travels.

It made me feel fine to be walking alone in the rain that day, alongside the tall, ordered rows of pines and birches, and I began to feel a kind of calm when I passed the townspeople. I couldn't have placed it then, but now, looking back, there was peace in the absence of talk. We passed, and our eyes would meet briefly, the sound of my boot heels amplified by cobblestones or alley walls. Then they would fall away from one another, our eyes, and they would know me by my skin, tan and sun-beat to linen, an American, no reason to speak, he will not understand the words, and I thought, Thank you, I am tired and do not know what to say. By then, in every instance, we had passed each other. And it felt good, somewhere behind my breastbone, to sense that this separation was explicable, a mere failing of language, and my loneliness could proceed with a different cause for a little while longer.

I reached a traffic circle where a pair of silver cabs idled. I tapped on the first one's driver-side window. The cabbie, a man with large eyes and a small, almost lipless mouth, sat up. He rolled his window down and leaned his head out ever so slightly. My hands were in the front pockets of my jeans and I leaned in to him as well. "K-town," I said quietly. For a moment we were very close, almost touching, and he said something that I didn't understand. "No sprechen," I said. He sighed and smiled and waved his hand toward the back-seat of his taxi and I got in.

And that's when it began, on that short ride in to Kaiserslautern. We rode in silence, without pleasantries, and the radio stayed off. I leaned my head against the window and watched as my breath condensed on it. I took my finger and made rudimentary lines in the fogged-over glass; first one, then another, until I had made the shape of a square, a smaller window inside the window. As I looked out onto the trees that edged the road, my muscles tensed and I began to sweat. I knew where I was: a road in Germany, AWOL, waiting for the flight back to the States. But my body did not: a road, the edge of it, and another day. My fingers closed around a rifle that was not there. I told them the rifle was not supposed to be there, but my fingers would not listen, and they kept closing around the space where my rifle was supposed to be and I continued to sweat and my heart was beating much faster than I thought reasonable.

I was supposed to be happy, but I cannot recall feeling much of anything except a dull, throbbing numbness. I was very tired and the blur of the silver trees on the side of the road became a comfort that described both newness and continuity at once. I wanted to get out and run my hands along the bark. I was sure that it was smooth and although it was still raining in the odd hovering way that it had been, I wanted to go out in it. To let it fall on my dark neck and hands, to feel it.

We rode the rest of the way into town like that, in silence, a few trembles held just so in my hands. He dropped me on a wide street. The sun hovered half hidden above the pale buildings in the rain. A few streetlights were on and gave off a thin glow through the gray afternoon, and after I paid the driver for the trip I began to walk toward the edge of town. I passed in and out of circles of light made by the sun through the clouds and the useless lamplight. By the time I reached the end of Turnerstrasse, the lights had adopted their own rhythm. My passage through them became more regular, something firm to which I could commit myself. I figured Sterling and some of the other guys would worm their way out to the bars to raise hell. I hoped I wouldn't see them, and not just because I'd gone AWOL. The mere thought of him made bile well up in a kind of raw, acidic burn at the back of my throat.

I passed a large cathedral on my right, and there was a dull cold in the air so I slipped inside. The interior of the cathedral was lit in a fashion that reflected the pale light outside its doors. I found a pamphlet in the foyer that gave the history of the church in German and in English, and I spread it out as wide as I could in an attempt to hide behind it. I ducked into a pew in the back of the church's transept. An after-school tour had started and although it was conducted in German, I tried to follow along as best I could from the pamphlet I held.

The cathedral was old. The sun had moved so that its light through the reds and blues of the high stained glass did not wash over the marble floor. It seemed to meet from both sides in the apse and in the nave, high up among the vaults and the old, carved capitals. The children's feet kicked dust into the air with little shuffles, and the dust hung in the light the special way it sometimes does.

In the far end of the church, behind the altar, a priest prepared for some ceremony. I watched him as he gathered candles and incense and arranged the items neatly on a small table behind him.

The tour guide stopped her group of children. She gestured to her mouth, then to her ears, then to her eyes. It was as if she had kissed her voice, her hearing and then her sight. We were all very still, the tour guide, the children and me, and the priest seemed to notice us because of the stillness. The children began moving along the walls, most giggling and playing grab-ass while others oohed and aahed at the portraits of the saints. I read the names of the saints from the pamphlet as the children walked, and I tried to imagine myself as a small child being introduced to them.

There was beautiful Sebastian, the arrows dangling from his chest. The blood from his injuries appeared like spattered candle-wax, hardened and congealed in a way that might allow a man to hang from a church wall unchanged and perpetually dying for a thousand years. There was Theresa, moaning like a woman brought to climax by the fire of her wounds. And there was Saint John Vianney, the incorruptible, the soldier who ran from Napoleon's army and heard confessions for twenty hours a day, whose heart rests separately in Rome, unadorned in a small glass case, undecayed and whole but for its absent beat.

In the cold interior of the cathedral the children oohed again. Their breath rose in one opaque breath, as it had risen in one small voice that hung above our heads briefly, obscuring the altar and the faint rose light that fell through the stained glass, and disappeared. I listened to the clicking of their small heels against the stone. I looked up toward the vaults, at the saint's picture frames, at the fine filigree that seemed to run like untended ivy through the place and read, "All that you see that is gold is truly gold." I said it to myself. I said it aloud. I looked down to read more, but there was nothing else. The pamphlet closed with those words.

As I read, the priest moved from his place behind the altar. I was surprised to see him standing over me when I folded the pamphlet down. He was small and wore wire-frame glasses and he looked at me and smiled with his mouth closed, the kind of smile that can be either empathetic or patronizing, depending on the person doing it. "You can't smoke in here," he said.

"What? Oh. Shit. Sorry." I hadn't even realized I'd lit up. The tip glowed red in the dim light until I snubbed it out on my boot and put it in my pocket.

"Can I help you with something?"

He must have thought my presence was an oddity. "No. I was just looking around. I'm on a pass," I lied.

He pointed to the pamphlet. "An interesting history, no?"

"Yeah. Yes," I stuttered, "it sure is."

He put his hand out. "I'm Father Bernard."

"Bartle. Private Bartle."

He sat down at the end of the pew, chuckled a bit and smoothed out the front of his pants. "I'm sort of a private, too, in a way."

I paused. "Oh, right," I said.

"Can I be honest with you?"

"Of course."

"You look troubled."

"Troubled?"

"Yes. Burdened."

"I don't know. I think I'm all right, I guess."

"I have some experience, you know. We could talk if you want."

"About what?" I asked.

"I thought you could decide that. I could listen."

I noticed I'd been cracking the knuckles on my left hand over and over again. "I don't know, Father. I don't really know how that stuff works. I'm not Catholic or anything."

He laughed. "You don't have to be Catholic. I made a promise that people could tell me things they didn't want to tell other people, that's all."

I had scratched the lacquer off a thin strip of the pew next to me. "I guess that's a good thing to do. What you do, I mean."

"They have an old saying about situations like this."

"What's that?"

"You are only as sick as your secrets."

"They got a saying about everything, don't they?"

"It's true." He smiled again.

I thought about it awhile. "You mean, like, I should make a confession or something."

"Well, not a, not a...just...talking."

"I just made a mistake is all."

"Everyone makes mistakes," he said.

"Nah," I said. "They don't. Not really."

The children and the tour guide had filed out of the cathedral. Light no longer fell through the windows and they looked like dark holes below the ceiling of the church in the dim lamp and candlelight.

I sat back in the pew and he sat at the end of the pew a little away from me and I thought how strange it was to be here, with the lights flickering, cold and wet. I felt foreign, acutely and overwhelmingly foreign. I felt an urge to run but didn't.

We both paused awkwardly. "I appreciate it, but I'd better be on my way. Thanks for your time, Father. If I'm not back soon I'll catch hell. Well, you know what I mean." I turned and began walking out of the transept and toward the large wooden doors at the front of the church. There was no noise other than my footsteps when the priest called out, "Do you want me to pray for you?"

I thought about what the priest asked and I looked around the cathedral. It was a beautiful place, the most beautiful I'd seen in a long time. But it was a sad kind of beauty, like all things created to cover the ugly reason they existed. I took the pamphlet out of my pocket. The entire history of the church was written there, three pages for a thousand years. Some poor fool had had to decide what was worth remembering, had had to lay it out neatly for whomever might come along to wonder. I had less and less control over my own history each day. I suppose I could have made some kind of effort. It should have been easy to trace: this happened, I was here, that happened next, all of which led inevitably to the present moment. I could have picked up a handful of dirt from the street outside, some wax from a candle on the altarpiece, ash from the incense as it swung past. I could have wrung it out, hoping I might find an essential thing that would give meaning to this place or that time. I did not. Certainty had surrendered all its territory in my mind. I'd have just been left with a mess in my hands anyway, no more. I realized, as I stood there in the church, that there was a sharp distinction between what was remembered, what was told, and what was true. And I didn't think I'd ever figure out which was which.

"No, sir. That's all right." I appreciated the gesture, but it seemed obligatory and somehow therefore meaningless, as all gestures come to seem.

"A friend, perhaps?"

"I had a friend. I have a friend you can pray for."

"Who is he?" the priest requested.

"Daniel Murphy. My battle. He got killed in Al Tafar. He died like…" I looked to the wall where the paintings of the saints hung. "It doesn't matter." The whole church was dark except for a few spheres of light that welled up from glowing candles and a few dim lamps.

Still, there went Murph, floating down toward that bend in the Tigris, where he passed beneath the shadow of the mound where Jonah was buried, his eyes just cups now for the water that he floated in, the fish having begun to tear his flesh already. I felt an obligation to remember him correctly, because all remembrances are assignations of significance, and no one else would ever know what happened to him, perhaps not even me. I haven't made any progress, really. When I try to get it right, I can't. When I try to put it out of my mind, it only comes faster and with more force. No peace. So what. I've earned it.

"And what should I pray?" he asked.

I thought of Sterling again. "Fuck 'em," I said under my breath. I turned back toward the priest. "Thanks, Father. You can pray whatever you want, I guess—whatever you don't think will be a waste of time."

I walked outside onto the cobblestone streets looking down at my feet. I am sure people noticed me, as I thought I heard a few gasps while I walked, but I never looked up. It wasn't in me. My separation was complete.

I walked aimlessly until I saw lamplight falling softly through the red curtains of a building near the outskirts of town. I heard music and women's voices coming through the thin openings above the windowsill. I hadn't particularly been looking for this place, but I remembered a cav scout in Al Tafar writing down the address for me on the torn top of a cigarette pack. "Best fucking place in history to get your dick wet. Fucking crucial," he'd said. Maybe I had intended to come here. I wanted something, something different, but I couldn't imagine that it would be getting my fucking dick wet. I lit a cigarette and stood in front of the building for several minutes. The rain continued to fall very gently over the city, and I was by this point nearly soaked through. Even the top part of my cigarette was wet and it burned unevenly and I had to take deep draws to keep it going in the rain.

It sounded like I could have a pleasant time inside, but crowds had already started to make me jumpy. If only Murph were here, I thought. But Murph was not there. Never would be. I was alone.

Maybe if things had happened a little differently in Al Tafar it could have been like that. But things happened the way they happened without regard to our desire for them to have happened another way. Despite an age-old instinct to provide an explanation more complex than that, something with a level of profundity and depth which would seem commensurate with the confusion I felt, it really was that simple.

Murph himself had told me that, as we stood over a field of worn and pale bodies scattered in the sun like driftwood. "If it ain't against the rules, it's mandatory," he'd muttered, mostly under his breath. He wasn't really talking to anyone in particular that day. He wasn't talking very much at all then, so I listened carefully when he did. I often thought about what he'd meant from that day on and it wasn't until I stood in front of the house with the light coming through the curtains that I understood. People have always done this, I thought. They looked for a curved road around the plain truth of it: an undetermined future, no destiny, no veined hand reaching into our lives, just what happened and our watching it. Knowing this was not enough, and I struggled to make it meaningful, as they had perhaps done here in Germany many years ago, looking for some pattern in all the strange things that occurred, covering their faces with ashes and pigments from berries they'd gathered from thawed valleys in spring, standing over the bodies of boys or women or old men covered by leaves or grasses ready to be lit beneath the stones that would hold them down in case the fires and the heat and the noise of the burning woke them from their strange sleep.

The door opened while I was distracted by my thoughts. A man walked out and pulled the brim of his hat down tightly around his face. When he saw me, he folded up the collar of his coat so that he appeared to be nothing more than a figure wrapped in fabric briskly walking down the road. The door was left open and I could see inside through the narrow opening. Women laughed and carried drinks around a parlor. A few men sat on pieces of worn furniture, wringing their hands and waiting for the women to bring drinks over to them and sit on their laps. When the women came, the men leaned their heads back and opened their arms wide to receive them. There was loud brass-band music coming from the house, and I followed it inside.

A small makeshift bar was shoved up against the far wall. I sat on one of the stools. Its leather upholstery was cracked and coming off in large swatches. A girl behind the bar spoke to me, but I could not understand her. It was loud inside, and she looked me up and down, and I remained in the seat without responding. Her hair was fine and red and even in the smoky room it seemed to shine with its own light. It looked artificially straightened, falling down not quite vertically on her shoulders, and I imagined smooth curls swinging as she moved. Her skin was pale and freckled, and a deep, purple bruise welled beneath her right eye.

"Whiskey?" I asked. I was alarmed at the softness and timidity of my own voice. It barely made its way through the smoke and music, but she seemed to hear me anyway. She went for a bottle on the top shelf. I shook my head and pointed down. "Lower," I said. She poured me a glass and I let it warm my throat and bite my stomach in a long swallow before I put it down. She never smiled at me. I watched her move around the room touching the arms of the business-men and teenagers that drank and waited for their turn with one of the other girls. I guessed that she was off from those duties tonight, maybe because of her black eye or for some other reason.

For a long time I was the only patron at the bar. When she was not pouring me another glass she would lean back against the wall and fold her pale arms across her small breasts. She did not look at me much and when she did and

I returned her gaze she would look away very quickly. Her blue eyes were rimmed with red and after a few glasses of whiskey I began to speak to her. "Are you all right?" I asked. I was beginning to slur.

She didn't answer me. The closest I got was when she would hold the bottle up and furrow her brow to see if I wanted another.

I heard a crash against the wall of the staircase. Coming down the steps, careening from wall to wall, was Sergeant Sterling. I wasn't really surprised. I couldn't have been the only Joe who'd heard about the place. He was shirtless and bleeding a little from the side of his mouth, and in his left hand he held a bottle of some clear liquor. The bottle flashed in the smoke and cold yellow light that fell from the naked bulbs swinging from the ceiling. When he saw me he bared his teeth and yelled, "Private Bartle!" I nearly slipped off the worn leather of the barstool. I could hear a few other people making noise upstairs and I saw Sterling as he staggered for a moment, the flash of recognition settling over his drunken face. I said a silent prayer that he would turn around and go back upstairs, but my prayers were futile, all of them, and I knew it. He came down and jerked a stool as close to mine as he could get it and his breathing was deep and ragged. The tattoos on his chest heaved with his breathing and he put his arm around my shoulders and squeezed hard. He was still smiling through his white teeth, and his eyes were wide and bloodshot and blue like the color of dried sprigs of lavender at the centers.

The bargirl had backed away from him when he came down the stairs, and he let go of me and lurched around the bar. "Not tonight?" he slurred at her. "Huh, bitch? Not tonight?" He grabbed her by the face with his free hand and squeezed and she struggled to get loose and I could see on her cheeks a deep red where he held her. His thumb and fingers made the skin of each opposing cheek sink between her teeth, and she tried to pull away. Tears ran down through the remains of her mascara, but she kept her fine jaw clenched and stood as tall and firmly as she could against the presence of his hands.

"Sergeant Sterling," I stammered. "Come have a drink with me." I could see that he heard me—a small twitching began behind his ears and the naked skin on the sides of his head bunched up ever so slightly—but he did not let her go. I pulled the stale air surrounding me deep into my lungs with a long breath and yelled, "Come on, pussy! Drink."

Before he let her go, he shoved her and her head hit the wall behind the bar and made a loud thump. The plaster cracked a little, and she started to run around the bar, but he caught her by her arm. He squeezed her elbow, forcing her arm straight. "Get back over there." She was crying softly to herself now and the red marks along her cheeks looked like a sad, painted-on clown smile and her mascara ran in black streaks below her eyes. He sat down next to me and slapped me on the back and grabbed me by the scruff of the neck. "Living the fucking dream, Private," he bellowed.

The room had long since cleared. Some of the customers had gone upstairs with girls, and others, not wanting to get caught up with a bunch of drunken Americans, had left and walked off into the night. The clock behind the bar read nearly two in the morning.

"This is complete freedom, hero." He laughed. "God, I love this."

The warm, astringent smell of the whiskey had begun to clean me out. Sterling sat quietly for a moment before he spoke. I lit a cigarette and the smoke from it hung above our heads in the yellow light. The girl slid her back down the wall and sat on the backs of her calves.

"Hey, you remember the look on his face when that hajji blew herself up at the DFAC?"

"Whose?" I asked.

"Murph's. C'mon, man. Murph's."

"Not really, Sarge. That day was fucked."

"Shit. That hajji was gone, Private. Poof. Gone." He put his arms around my neck and squeezed. "Poof. Gone."

"Yeah."

"He had a really funny look on his face."

"I can't remember."

"I thought you remembered everything. Like some retarded genius or something."

I tried to laugh it off. "You're wasted, Sarge," I said.

"Yeah. But now you see how shit ends up?"

"Sure. Yeah. Sure I do."

"I'm in charge."

I laughed nervously. "I know that."

"When I'm in charge, things end up OK. When I let people talk me into shit...we are a fucking no-go at this station."

I tried to change the subject. "What made you think of Murph?"

"Fuck Murph."

I didn't say anything.

"We know what happened. That's all we got."

He was drunk. I'd never seen him like that: on the edge of losing control, morose and somehow sentimental in his own way. It was like you could feel him about to shake loose from something, I wasn't sure what from, but I didn't want to be around when it happened.

He put his finger into my chest and then into his. "We know. Me and you. Like we're married. Don't you forget. I've fucking got you, Private Bartle. UC motherfucking MJ, anytime I want. You see this?" He took his thumb and held it in my face, pushing his fist firmly and deliberately against my cheek. He then turned his hand and pressed his thumb into the dark lacquered wood of the bar top, grinding it against the surface as if squishing a bug. "That's where you are. I own you. And AWOL, too? Too fucking easy, Private."

I'd be out soon. My three-year enlistment was up. I was getting out of the army when we got back stateside. "You won't do it," I said. I didn't really believe it. I knew Sterling was capable of anything. "I can give you up too. You were in charge, remember?"

"Ah," he grunted. "No one gives a fuck about Murph," he said. When he reached the fricative in Murph's name, he began to laugh. I could feel his breath on my lips. As he talked, his eyes flashed a little and the color of them seemed to wash out and deaden. "Everybody else, man, they don't want to know. If they wanted to, they would, right? It's not like he's the only bullshit KIA with bullshit medals and a bullshit story for his mother?" He drained the last of the liquor from his bottle, tipping it up slowly above his head. I watched his Adam's apple move the clear liquor down his throat. When he finished, he threw the bottle against the wall above the bargirl's head. It did not shatter. The thick glass held and it made a sharp thwack against the wall and fell.

"We could tell," I said. "Just get the whole thing over with."

He laughed. "There you go again, Private. Retarded genius."

I woke upstairs. I was in a bed, two mattresses on top of each other, really. The paper on the walls was striped yellow and corroded white and peeling. I heard running water from down the hall. I could see the bargirl's reflection in the dirty mirror through an open door. A few seconds passed before I recognized her. She came out of the bathroom in a dingy pink robe. I saw freckles scattered over her chest, down her arms, down her long pale legs.

"Is he gone?" I asked her.

She took a damp washcloth and pressed it onto my forehead. I felt sick. "Yes," she said.

"You speak English."

"Of course I do."

I couldn't identify her accent. Tracks on her arms. No saint. Me neither. I saw that the bruise below her eye had deepened. It was now a thick black. I lay back on the bed. "I'm sorry," I told her. "I should have done something else."

"You tried. That's something."

"Will you…," I began. I didn't know what I wanted from her.

She cut me off. "Are you serious?" A very sad look came over her face and her bottom lip began to tremble slightly and she slapped me.

"No. Not that," I said, although a part of me did want to, to have control over something, even if it was for just two minutes. But I disgusted myself. I thought of the Joe who'd given me the address. He had probably done it, and he was probably dead. I imagined his body collapsing in on itself, the flesh rotting and then gone, the skin on his lips cracked until only dust remained in a thin veneer over his skull. I pushed her hands up to my withers. I moved them back and forth against the very short hair on the side of my head. I doubled over and grabbed an old metal trash can next to the bed and threw up into it. She rubbed my back. She kneeled at the foot of the bed and I sat up.

"You are all so sad," she said.

I noticed an odd chirping outside the bedroom windows and I saw a few starlings flit by in the pale light of the street-lamps. They flew in circles, or else there were many of them, and the whole group passed in and out of the light on their way to settle on a rooftop, or on some tree that asked to have its branches filled, at least until its leaves and flowers blossomed, until winter was as far away as it could be. We stayed like that awhile. I finally let go of her thin waist and looked at her. "Is everyone gone?" I asked.

She nodded.

"I'll go back downstairs and sleep there if that's OK."

"Yes, fine."

I was still quite drunk and my head was foggy. I went behind the bar and found a whiskey bottle. I sat on the floor and looked out the window and drank the rest of the whiskey. The sun came up over a small canal across the street. I was very tired, looking out over the narrow band of water, wondering if it was cold.

The light was graying when I opened my eyes. The street-lights were still on. There was a bitter taste in my mouth. I looked around to get my bearings. My head pounded. My hands were very cold, and I realized I was lying facedown on the bank of the thin canal with my hands dangling in the water. It was flat and glassy and the only motion on the water was where my hands moved in it slightly. I pulled them out and sat up and began to rub my hands together to get the feeling in them back. God, what time is it? I thought. The house was across the street. The women stood like tired caryatids on the porch, each one leaning against one or another of several warped and peeling columns. They did not move, and I stood up and turned toward them, and they remained that way, as if in some raw tableau.

"Where is the girl?" I hollered.

They stood the way they had been for another moment, and then they turned and filed through the door. It was quiet inside or seemed to be, and I stood there staring at the house until I realized it must have been close to dawn.

When I got back to the base, the LT was angry. He didn't yell, he just said, "Wash up, Bartle." I did and when I was finished I changed into a clean uniform and pulled a field jacket over my shoulders and fell asleep on a bench in the terminal. Only a few MPs and officers were still awake.

I was woken by a nudge on my shoulder, then by a harder shake. I rolled over, and Sergeant Sterling whispered to me, "I covered for you."

"Thanks, Sarge," I said groggily.

"Don't go thinking we're finished, Private." He walked away. Outside in the dark it had begun to rain again. I was almost home, I thought, almost gone.

4

SEPTEMBER 2004

Al Tafar, Nineveh Province, Iraq

THROUGH THE DAYLIGHT hours we took turns on watch, sleeping for two hours and nodding off behind our rifles for one. We saw no enemy. We made up none out of the corners of our eyes. We were too tired even for that. We saw only the city, appearing as a blurred patchwork of shapes sketched in white and tan beneath a ribbon of blue sky.

I woke for my shift as the sun set into a wadi. It snaked off beyond the orchard, cut into the foothills and disappeared. The fires in the orchard had gone out, but Murph and I did not notice their absence until we heard the thin crackling of embers gently smoldering in the distance. The shadows of the outbuildings reached down and covered everything and we didn't notice it was happening and then it was night.

We'd gotten lax. The LT rarely asked us to dig in, and we hadn't dug in there, just laid our packs and rifles against the lurching clay-mud walls that separated that cluster of buildings from the field we'd been fighting over for the last few nights. The LT had a small antenna radio, and a green mosquito net hung between an open window and a half-charred hawthorn tree. We waited for him to tell us something, but he had his feet up on a field table and seemed to be sleeping so we let him rest.

A runner from battalion headquarters brought us our mail after chow. He had on thick glasses and smiled at us and took great care to duck below walls and trees, which looked, to him, like cover. His uniform was very clean. When he whispered out Murph's name, Murph thanked him and smiled up at him and opened the letter and began to read. The runner handed me a small package, and Sergeant Sterling stood up from behind his cover, a stack of sawed-off trunks of pear trees that some long-vanished family must have placed there, stacked up to be ready to burn through the cold nights of winter where the plains met the foothills of the Zagros and it sometimes snowed.

Sterling called the runner over to him. "Private," he barked, "where's my mail?"

"It doesn't look like you got any."

"Sergeant," Sterling muttered.

"Excuse me?"

"Relax, Sterling, give the kid a break," the LT said, awake now and pausing from his conversation on the radio. It was the only sound. The runner pushed his body toward the lowering dark in silence, seeming to float above the packed dust as he moved back the way he came.

Murph took a photograph from his helmet and placed it over the letter, using it to cover the words that would come next, giving each line its due attention, the way that old men do when reading obituaries of friends, learning late the small measures of their lives and wondering how it was they came to not know these things. It was too dark to see the picture from where I sat. I didn't remember Murph ever showing it to me. I wondered how we'd gone that long through the war without my having seen it. He rested his back against the wall, and the low-hanging branches of the hawthorn tree reached down to him in the quiet wind. The reds of the setting sun had washed out and the last soft hint of pink disappeared behind the city.

"Good news?" I asked.

"News, anyway," he said.

"What's up?"

"My girlfriend's going to school. Says she figures the best thing is…well, you know."

The radio continued to buzz softly. The LT's voice draped down over our whispers, saying, "They're good boys. They'll be ready, Colonel."

"Jody's got your girl?" I asked him.

"I don't know. I don't think so."

"You all right?"

"Yeah. Don't matter, I guess."

"Sure?"

There was no sound between my question and his answer. I thought of home, remembering the cicadas fluttering their wings in the scrub pines and oaks that ringed the pond behind my mother's house outside Richmond. It would be morning there. The space between home, whatever that might mean for any of us, and the scratched-out fighting positions we occupied, collapsed. Soon, I looked out over the water. I smiled. I remembered late Novembers. Needles browned by the warm Virginia air collecting like discarded blankets on the shore. Taking the warped steps down from the back of the house on the cusp of morning, the sun slouching behind the tallest trees on the hills above the draw where our house sat. The light strong and yellow and thin, appearing to raise itself out of the earth, invisible, up from some higher plane where as a child I imagined there must be fields of cut grass and thistle that glowed until the day had again assured them of its presence, and my mother reading on the porch so early in the morning, seeming not to notice me as I walked past, my feet making a pleasant noise as they slid through the orange and yellow leaves. It would be too dark for my mother to see me. Out all night after I enlisted. I recalled telling her just like that. Trying to sneak into the backyard through the gate in the post fence my brother built, how she called out softly, not waiting for her breath to catch up to her voice, and it took me a minute to hear her, as the bullfrogs bellowed through their last darkening songs. A little wind came up and scattered those birds that always seemed to gather in the far cove beneath the willows and dogwoods that claimed that corner of the bank's good brown earth. When they flew, they broke the water with the tips of their spanned wings, and the light from the house and a few stars like handfuls of salt thrown out appeared to break as well, and the ripples on the pond wavered as though the lines across the water were plucked strings. But I wasn't there. All that had happened a long time before. I'd walked up in the dark under the awning of a few trees and she'd said, knowing somehow the way mothers always seem to, "My God, John, what did you do?" And I'd said I joined up. She knew what that meant. It wasn't much longer before I'd left. I couldn't remember having a life at all between that day and where I sat beneath a wall that ringed a field in Al Tafar, unable to reassure my friend, who would soon be dead. He was right. It hadn't mattered.

Murph paused. "Everything's just so goddamn funny." He had the letter folded in his lap, and he bent his head backward, and the outline of his face was oriented toward the sky. He made a childish connection, but a beautiful one, and his face, looking through the thin fingers of the hawthorn that rose out of the dust, seemed to connect the long black veil of sky above us, a few stars in its stitching, to whatever sky his girl sat beneath. And yes, it was full of naïveté and boyishness, but that is all right, because we were boys then. It makes me love him a little, even now, to remember him sitting beneath the hawthorn tree, sad that his girl had left him, but without anger or resentment, despite being only a few hours removed from all the killing of the night before. He sat there in the dark. We spoke like children. We looked at each other as if into a dim mirror. I remember that part of him fondly, before he was lost, before he surrendered fully to the war, twisting through the air, perhaps one beat of his heart remaining as they threw his tortured body from the window of the minaret.

I put out my hand and gestured for him to hand me the picture. It was a Polaroid of Murph and his girl. They stood on a dirt track. The earth rose behind them, up out of the picture toward its promontory. The mountain was covered by beech and magnolia, white ash and maple, tulip trees, and all the colors of the flowers were bright and definite in the rays of light that settled down through the upper branches. She wore a dress of blue-dyed muslin that had been worn thin, and the light in the picture passed through the thin fabric slightly, revealing the shape of her body. Her hair was brown and a little stringy and in the picture a few strands came to rest on her high, pink cheeks. Her mouth was closed. She did not smile and her eyes were gray and warm above a hand that looked as if it was captured on its way to brush stray hairs from her face.

Then Murph next to her. His hands in the pockets of his blue jeans. Her other hand on the small of his back. Alive. There was an expression on his face that I have never seen before or since. I have convinced myself that this was the expression of one who knew, but he could not have. There was something fleeting in the picture, though I didn't know it then. He had an easy half smile, and his eyes squinted in the light. What was there of permanence in the picture? I wondered if the girl would ever stand on that spot again. If she did, would she reach for the small of his back?

"Who took it?"

He squatted on the back of his calves, pulling a rub out and putting it in his bottom lip. The smell was sweet and pungent and filled the calm air. "My mom did, summer before last. I guess we were sixteen, almost seventeen in it. Marie's a good girl. I can't say I blame her. Too smart to stick with me."

Sterling had been listening to us talk. He loped over out of the dark on the other side of the tree. "I'd kill a bitch," he interjected. "You're not really gonna take that shit, are you, Private?"

"I guess I figure it's not my call to make no more, Sarge."

Sterling put his hands on his hips and seemed to be waiting for Murph to say something else. It was as if that line of words had been hung up in a place Sterling couldn't reach, so he just stood there, disregarding, waiting to be readdressed. But Murph did not respond. Neither did I. We just looked at him, half leaning against the wall. Behind us a streetlamp came on. It was the only one to survive the battle, and it illuminated the field where the dead lay scattered and it shined its light briefly into the scarred earth where the mortars had fallen. It flickered. In the intermittent light Sterling seemed to flicker also, appearing and disappearing. The light went out for a short stretch, and Sterling walked away.

I want him to resist now, as I remember it. Not like Sterling suggested, but to resist nonetheless. It wasn't that I thought he should have hoped that his being abandoned could be changed, but I wanted something that I could look back on and say, yes, you were fighting too, you burned to be alive, and whatever failure or accident of nature caused you to be killed could be explained by something other than the fact that I'd missed your giving up.

Murph looked at me and shrugged his shoulders. I handed him back the picture of Marie, and he took his helmet off, resting it between his legs in the dust. He took out his casualty feeder card from a ziplock bag under his helmet liner and put the picture behind it. He held the card and the picture and looked at them in the unsteady light, and I read the sections of the card that Murph had already filled in.

At the top of the card, in the appropriate boxes, Murph had written the requested information. His name: Murphy, Daniel; his social security number; his rank; his unit. Below that were other boxes, left blank in case the need arose to record an assortment of information with a quick X in ink. There was a box for Killed in Action, for Missing in

Action, and for Wounded in Action (either lightly or seriously). There was a box for Captured, and for Detained, and for Died as a Result of Wounds. There were two sets of Yes or No boxes, one each for Body Recovered and Body Identified. There was a space for witness remarks and for the signature of the commanding officer or medical personnel. Murph had placed an X in the box for Body Recovered. "Just in case," he said when he caught me looking. Both of our cards were signed already.

Murph folded the picture up with the card and put them both back under his helmet liner. I cut open my package and pulled out a bottle of Gold Label sent by one of my high school buddies. I shook the bottle gently back and forth, saying, "Look what we got here." He smiled and put his helmet to the side and he slid along the wall to get a little closer to me. I put my hand out with the bottle and he waved me off.

"I believe you have the honor, sir."

We both laughed. I took a long pull of the whiskey. It burned inside my nose and down my throat and down into my stomach. I had to wipe the back of my hand across my mouth because we were laughing. Murph took the bottle and took a long swallow. For a moment we forgot our predicament and were just two friends drinking under a tree, leaned up against a wall, trying to muffle our laughter so we would not get caught. Murph stifled his laughter until his body was racked with deep spasms that caused his armor to rattle, grenades to softly tinkle against one another, until all the accoutrements of battle jingled slightly and he had to stop himself, repeating, "All right, I'm good," with a mock stone face until he had regained his bearing. When he handed me back the bottle he sighed deeply. "Look out over there."

Murph pointed to the low hills around the city. Small fires had sprung up in the distance. A few city lights and the fires on the hillsides burned like a tattered quilt of fallen stars. "It's beautiful," I whispered. I was not sure if anyone heard me, but I saw others point their fingers off into the darkness.

We stayed like that for a while. The night grew cool and the smell of the fires burning was bright and clean and cut through the air like a spring wind out of season. I started to feel a little drunk as we traded the bottle back and forth. We rested our chins on our arms and our arms on the top of the low mud-brick wall and we watched the little fires the citizens made speckle the hillsides in every direction.

"It must be the whole city out there," Murph said, and I thought of the line of people who rode or walked or ran out of Al Tafar four days ago, how they waited patiently for us to leave, for the enemy to leave, how when the battle was over they would come back and begin to sweep the shells off the roofs of their houses, how they would fill buckets of water and splash them over the dried, coppery blood on their doorsteps. We could hear a soft keening while we watched the low hills and desert glimmer in the darkness.

It was barely perceptible, that noise. I still hear it sometimes. Sound is a funny thing, and smell. I'll light a fire in the back lot of my cabin after the sun goes down. Then after a while, the smoke settles down into little ruts between clumps of pine. Wind whips up through the draws nearby and courses over the creek bed. And I can hear it then. I was not sure if it really came from the women around the campfires, if they pulled their hair crying out in mourning or not, but I heard it and even now it seems wrong not to listen. I took off my helmet and placed my rifle on top of it and allowed my ears to adjust to the ambient sounds in the night. There was something out there. I glanced at Murph and he returned a sad and knowing look. The LT put the radio down and sat in his chair with his head in his hands rubbing the strange mark on his cheekbone. We all listened to it awhile, watching the fires burn against the night. My chest tightened. There was something both ordinary and miraculous about the strange wailing that we heard, and the way it carried to us on the wind that began inside the orchard. Later in the night two of the lights in the distance began to brighten, then another two, and then another. The LT walked to each of us and said, "The colonel wants to see you guys. Get ready."

We put our rifles out over the wall and gripped the forestocks tightly. We put out our cigarettes and asserted ourselves against the silence beyond our small encampment. I felt like a self-caricature, that we were falsely strong. When we spoke, we spoke brusquely and quietly and deepened our voices.

The lights formed a more regular line and we began to hear the whine of motors and then the lights disappeared and a cloud of dust rolled toward us above the ground from the front of the building near the road. The LT moved around our defensive perimeter and softly called out to us, "Stay alert. Stay alive."

Two young sergeants quickly moved from around the building and spread out to either end of the wall. Then the colonel came, short, red-haired and walking upright as tall as he could. He had a reporter and a cameraman with him. The LT exchanged a few words with him and they both turned to us. "How's the war tonight, boys?" he asked. A broad smile spread over his face in the darkness.

"Good," Sterling replied with a dull certainty.

As if in need of confirmation, the colonel slowly met each of us eye to eye until we'd all said, "Yes, sir, it's good tonight."

Even in the intermittent light the crispness of his uniform was clearly visible. He smelled of starch when he came close to us. He folded his arms across his chest and began to speak, and the smile on his face disappeared. I briefly wondered which face was the real one before he pulled out a piece of paper and began to read from it, pausing ever so slightly to make sure the reporter was paying attention, "Are you rolling?"

"Go ahead. Pretend we're not here."

The colonel cleared his throat and pulled a pair of glasses out of his pocket and rested them on the bridge of his nose.

One of the sergeants came over and shined a small flashlight on the colonel's piece of paper. "Boys," he began, "you will soon be asked to do great violence in the cause of good." He paced back and forth and his boot prints in the fine dust were never trampled. Each step was precise and his pacing only served to firm and define the tracks that he originally left. The sergeant with the flashlight paced beside him. "I know I don't have to tell you what kind of enemy you'll be up against." His voice became a blunt staccato as he gained confidence in his capacity to motivate us, a bludgeon that smoothed the weary creases in my brain. "This is the land where Jonah is buried, where he begged for God's justice to come." He continued, "We are that justice. Now, I wish I could tell you that all of us are coming back, but I can't. Some of you will not come back with us." I was moved then, but what I now recall most vividly about that speech was the colonel's pride, his satisfaction with his own directness, his disregard for us as individuals. "If you die, know this: we'll put you on the first bird to Dover. Your families will have a distinction beyond all others. If these bastards want a fight, we're going to give them one." He paused. A look of great sentimentality came over him. "I can't go with you boys," he explained with regret, "but I'll be in contact from the operation center the whole time. Give 'em hell."

The LT started a round of applause. We'd been told to maintain noise and light discipline, but that had all gone out the window with the camera crew and the colonel's half-assed Patton imitation. I could tell the colonel was dis-appointed. I looked at the rest of the platoon to see if I could read anything on their faces. Murph gazed down at the toes of his boots. Sterling listened attentively on a knee from un-derneath the hawthorn tree. The fires in the dark became lights that fluttered on the backs of my closed eyelids.

The colonel gestured toward the LT, extending his arm out to him, palm up. "Lieutenant, they are all yours."

"Thank you, sir." He cleared his throat three times. "All right, boys, we'll be on fifty-percent security tonight. We move from this position just before light, crossing the open ground out there while we still have the cover of darkness." There were a few glances over shoulders into the barren space between our position and the city proper. It was far too dark to see into it, but the images were there like an etching through the night. The stench of the dead had cut itself free from the other odors coming from Al Tafar. The trash fires and sewage, the heavy scent of cured lamb, the river; above all this was the stink of decay from the bodies themselves. A shudder ran through my shoulders, a quick shake, as I hoped not to step into the slick mess of one of them as we marched to the fight. "We'll clear the open ground and pass along the road that swings around the city, using the buildings on the outskirts for cover. When we get to the orchard, we'll spread out along this ditch here." He pointed to a map illuminated by a pale green glow stick. It showed a narrow scratch in the earth, buildings crowded behind it, not forty yards from the first trees in the orchard. "Any questions?"

"What then?" someone asked.

The LT glanced timidly at the colonel, bit his lip and said, "They're in there. We're going in there."

Then it was quiet. It seemed we were all measuring the distances we'd travel in the morning. The bends in the road between corners of buildings, a low wall here, there an up-ended dumpster we could use for cover. The heights of the trees, low enough so we'd enter the orchard hunching, passing through leaves once heavy with citrus and olive, the trees planted in rows so orderly that we thought we'd have clear views from one end of the world to the other. But the orchard was much too large for that. We didn't know that yet because we hadn't seen it from the inside. It filled dozens of acres between two spurs of bald, grassy earth that drooped down toward the city. The ground in the little valley lay flat in spots, heaved up in others, the whole of it covered by the old growth of fruit trees and two or three times grafted branches.

The colonel's voice snapped up our attention. "We're gonna drop mortars in that rathole for two hours before dawn. They'll still be shredding those little trees right when you get up to 'em. We're counting on you, boys. The people of the United States are counting on you. You may never do anything this important again in your entire lives."

He hupped the two sergeants and the embedded

reporters he'd brought with him, and they pulled off from the wall and trotted back to the front of the building. We heard his vehicle start. I heard him ask the reporter how the shots looked and then he was gone.

"Damn," Murph said.

"What?"

"You think this is really the most important thing we'll ever do, Bartle?"

I exhaled. "I hope not."

The LT sat down in his chair again. The low crackle and hum of the radio was back on. The wind seemed to pick up a little and we watched the fires again in the hills. He looked scared and tired and he rubbed the small blemish on his face with the tips of two fingers. I forget most of the time that he was only a few years older than the rest of us, twenty-three or twenty-four, I'd guess. I never took the time to ask. He appeared older, though, like Sterling, and carried himself that way, or maybe we just granted him extra years because he'd done things we hadn't: drunk at college parties with girls wild enough to run back into a strange room on a dare from their friends, driven a brand-new car.

"How many times have we been through that orchard, through this town, sir?" a PFC from third squad asked.

"The army?"

"Yes, sir."

"This makes three."

"All in the fall?"

"Yeah, seems like we're fighting over this town every year."

I thought of my grandfather's war. How they had destinations and purpose. How the next day we'd march out under a sun hanging low over the plains in the east. We'd go back into a city that had fought this battle yearly; a slow, bloody parade in fall to mark the change of season. We'd drive them out. We always had. We'd kill them. They'd shoot us and blow off our limbs and run into the hills and wadis, back into the alleys and dusty villages. Then they'd come back, and we'd start over by waving to them as they leaned against lampposts and unfurled green awnings while drinking tea in front of their shops. While we patrolled the streets, we'd throw candy to their children with whom we'd fight in the fall a few more years from now.

"Maybe they'll make it an annual thing," Murph snapped.

Sterling came over from around the hawthorn where he had cleaned and loaded his weapons and taped down loose and moving parts so that they would not rattle. "Check me out, little man," he told Murph. He jumped up and down, his hands at his sides. Silence. The only sound he made was the soft humph of his boots tamping down the fine dust. "All right. Good. Bartle, come over here, please."

I moved over toward Sterling and Murph and watched as Sterling placed black electrical tape over the shiny, metallic pieces of gear that could protrude and reflect a glint of light in through a window in the predawn as we walked. Murph stood there motionless, and Sterling adjusted his equipment firmly and carefully. The look on his face was one of care. He bit at his lip, furrowed up his brow and turned the corners of his mouth down ever so slightly. When he was finished he rubbed his hands along the length of Murph's body, almost caressing him. "Give it a shot," he said.

Murph looked over to me and jumped off the ground a little and nothing moved or made a noise.

"Your turn, Bartle."

He repeated the process for me, the same look of concern marking his face. When I jumped, there was no sound and Sterling patted me on the side of the helmet.

"Sarge," I asked, "do you think we're gonna have to fight here every year?"

"Hell yes, Private," he said. "I was already in the first one. This shit's gonna be bigger than Ohio State–Michigan." He chuckled. He could tell I was nervous again. "Don't worry. We're gonna do all right tomorrow, OK? Just follow me, do what I say, and we'll be back on the FOB before you know it."

He smiled at both of us. He seemed to soften in the strange light from the lamppost. "OK, Sarge. Sure. We'll follow you all the way."

In the morning we woke to the narrow whine of mortars as they arced over our position and crumpled into the orchard. It remained dark. The sky was the color of brittle charcoal. What always happened to me before a fight happened then: a feeling I'd never felt until I went to the high desert to fight. Every time it came I searched for something to make the knot in my chest make sense, to help me understand the tremble that took over my thighs and made my fingers slick and clumsy. Murph once came close to describing it. A reporter had asked us what combat felt like. He'd worn a khaki outfit festooned with pockets and mirror-lens aviator glasses that could blind you from a hundred yards away. We hated having him around, but we'd been ordered to tolerate him, so when he came up to a group of us lounging in the dust beneath a large shade tree on base, saying, "Tell me the essence, guys, I want to know the kind of rush you get," most of us ignored him, a few told him to go fuck himself, but Murph tried to explain. He said, "It's like a car accident. You know? That instant between knowing that it's gonna happen and actually slamming into the other car. Feels pretty helpless actually, like you've been riding along same as always, then it's there staring you in the face and you don't have the power to do shit about it. And know it. Death, or whatever, it's either coming or it's not. It's kind of like that," he continued, "like that split second in the car wreck, except for here it can last for goddamn days." He paused. "Why don't you come out with us and you can take point? I'll bet you'll find out." The reporter left after that, something in the way we laughed made him stutter and backpedal out of our platoon area. But Murph was right about the feeling, and every time it began my body told me it couldn't sustain the tightened muscles and sweat. But it didn't end, so I tried not to pay attention to it.

"Noise and light discipline from here on out, boys," the LT whispered. I was glad not to be out on the point. The guy who was swung his leg over the low wall separating our position from the open field and walked out toward the gray shapes of the city.

Sterling took a small canister of salt out of his ruck while we waited for our squad's turn to move out. I remember that there was a picture of a girl with an umbrella on the label. Morton's, I think. He turned the cylinder over and began to shake it over the earth beneath the hawthorn tree. I looked at Murph, and he returned my questioning expression, and we walked toward Sterling. "Uh, Sarge, are you all right?" Murph asked. Sterling spread the salt over the ground where we'd been set up the night before.

"It's from Judges," he said, without really noticing us. Then he looked up and seemed to look past us, out into the end of the night, which somewhere over the horizon line prepared to reveal itself as day. "Move out, guys," he said. "It's just a thing I do." So we did. In the distance behind us Sterling walked, just barely in sight, spreading salt over the fields and alleys, over the dead bodies and into the dust that seemed to cover everything in Al Tafar. He spread it wherever he went, the whole time singing or muttering in a voice neither of us had ever heard him use before. It was a pleasant voice, friendly, and although we couldn't make out the words, it terrified us.

"I think he's losing his shit, Bart," Murph said.

"You want to tell him?" I asked.

The mortars still fell. A few times a minute we twitched from the noise of the loud impacts like kettledrums banging in the orchard. Small fires burned. The smoke rose from among the frayed leaves. Once, when it was nearly light, Murph said, "I'm gonna see what Sterling's up to." He raised his rifle to use the magnification scope to look back at him.

"Well?"

There was a brief flash of light as the first faint rays crested the foothills to the east and fell along the roofs and walls of the buildings' pale facades. I looked back and put my hand up on my brow line trying to focus on his figure, barely perceptible in the receding dark. "Well?" I repeated, "What is he doing?"

The figure in the distance was motionless. Perhaps all the salt was spread along this short stretch of the outskirts of Al Tafar. We were very close to the orchard and my legs were still quivering with fear. "Murph, what's he doing?"

He lowered the rifle. His mouth was open. He closed it, then spoke. "I don't know, man. He's got a fucking body." Murph looked at me, wide-eyed. "And he's not smiling anymore."

5

MARCH 2005

Richmond, Virginia

CLOUDS SPREAD OUT over the Atlantic like soiled linens on an unmade bed. I knew, watching them, that if in any given moment a measurement could be made it would show how tentative was my mind's mastery over my heart. Such small arrangements make a life, and though it's hard to get close to saying what the heart is, it must at least be that which rushes to spill out of those parentheses which were the beginning and the end of my war: the old life disappearing into the dust that hung and hovered over Nineveh even before it could be recalled and longed for, young and unformed as it was, already broken by the time I reached the furthest working of my memory. I was going home. But home, too, was hard to get an image of, harder still to think beyond the last curved enclosure of the desert, where it seemed I had left the better portion of myself as one among innumerable grains of sand, how in the end the weather-beaten stone is not one stone but only that which has been weathered, a result, an example of slow erosion on a thing by wind or waves that break against it, so that the else of anyone involved ends up deposited like silt spilling out into an estuary, or gathered at the bottom of a river in a city that is all you can remember.

The rest is history, they say. Bullshit, I say. It's imagination or it's nothing, and must be, because what is created in this world, or made, can be undone, unmade; the threads of a rope can be unwoven. And if that rope is needed as a guideline for a ferry to a farther shore, then one must invent a way to weave it back, or there will be drownings in the streams that cross our paths. I accept now, though in truth it took some time, that *must* must be its own permission.

Forgiveness is an altogether different thing. It can't be patterned, as a group of boys can become a calculus for what will go ungrieved, the shoulders slumping in the seats of a chartered plane, the empty seats between them, how if God had looked on us during that flight back home we might have seemed like fabric ready to be thrown, in the surrendered blankness of our sleep, over the furniture of a thousand empty houses.

I'd been looking out the window for a glimpse of the ocean ever since the plane's wheels left the ground. A dull cheer rolled from the first-class cabin back to the rear of the plane where the enlisted men sat. The huff of breath that exited our bodies became a grasp at joy when the plane dipped into the air and separated from the earth. The officers and senior enlisted men turned over the backs of their broad chairs, waved their hands and yelled, and we began to yell and smile, slowly, as if our bodies were underwater.

The plane reached cruising altitude. The flight from Germany to the States was relatively short. The Atlantic Ocean was our last obstacle to home, the land of the free, of reality television, outlet malls and deep vein thrombosis. I woke with my head against the window, unaware that I'd been sleeping. My hand went to close around the stock of the rifle that was not there. An NCO from third platoon sitting across the aisle saw it and smiled. "Happened to me twice today," he said. I did not feel better.

I looked at the battalion scattered throughout the plane. How many didn't make it? Murph. Three specialists from Bravo company who'd been killed by a suicide bomber in the chow hall. A few others scattered over the year. One from HQ company killed by a mortar on the FOB. Another I didn't know but had heard was killed by a sniper. Ten more? Twenty?

Those that remained were dark against the blue seats and thin squares of blanket covering them. They twitched and grunted and rolled within the confines of their business-class chairs. I looked out the window and saw that it was not yet night despite the fact that my body had sensed its coming a few hours before. We traveled with the sun, uncoupled from its dictates of light and dark for a little while. I watched the broad ocean spread out beneath me after the clouds thinned. I focused for what seemed like hours on crests becoming troughs, troughs tilting to become whitecaps, all of it seeming like the breaking of some ancient treaty between all those things that stand in opposition to one another.

A group of clerks who remained awake had taken to ringing their assistance bells incessantly so that the attendants would be forced to make their rounds and lean into them, the smell of lilac and vanilla descending heavily from their tanned chests. The older ones performed this task by rote, pushed wide their shoulders, showed skin like browned wax paper.

The clerks must have tired of their game after a while because it grew quiet. Only the deliberate hum of the engines filled my ears. I began the same thought over and over as we breached the sand and rock and thistle of the coast, but could not complete it. I want to go...I want to...I want...I...and then the coast greened as we flew farther inland. The earth was pocked with blue pools, the brown squares of ball fields and mazes of houses arrayed like strange reproductions of themselves. And green. It was impossibly green. There seemed to be trees growing out of every inch of the land. It was spring and some bloomed and from this height even the blooms were green and it was so green that I would have jumped from the plane if I could have, to float over that green briefly, to let it be real and whole and as large as I imagined. And as I thought of my descent, how I would take in that last breath of green before I scattered over the earth, I remembered the last word — home. I want to go home.

"Wake up. We're here," the LT said. I looked out the window and saw a sign left open to flap and tatter in the wind outside the terminal. It thanked us for our service and welcomed us back to the States.

That was it. The doors opened and we lurched down the gangway toward the bright shine of the airport. It glowed on the inside, and the curl of small neon letters against white walls and white floors addled my thinking. My mind clouded over. I saw a nation unfold in the dark. It rolled out over piedmont and hillock and fell down the west face of the Blue Ridge, where plains in pink dusk rested softly under an accretion of hours. Between the coasts, an unshared year grew like goldenrod and white puffs of dandelion up through the hardpan.

We filed in through a special gate and stood in the cold wash of the artificial lights and listened to them buzz and hum. A few last words from the officers and senior enlisted men and then we would be released. The usual had become remarkable, the remarkable boring, and toward whatever came in between I felt only a listless confusion.

The LT gave a safety brief. Standard stuff: "Wrap it up. Don't drink and drive. If your old lady is pissing you off, remember..."

We answered in unison, "Instead of a slug, give her a hug." We'd stood tightly in formation until the first sergeant barked "Dismissed," but we did not scatter in all directions at once. Instead, the remains of our unit dissolved slowly, scattering from its center the way a splash of oil might over water. I saw confusion in some of the other soldiers' eyes. I even heard a few say, "Well, what now?" It crossed my own mind, too, but I put my fingernails into my palms until the skin broke, and I thought, No way, no goddamn way, something else now.

The ghosts of the dead filled the empty seats of every gate I passed: boys destroyed by mortars and rockets and bullets and IEDs to the point that when we tried to get them to a medevac, the skin slid off, or limbs barely held in place detached, and I thought that they were young and had girls at home or some dream that they thought would make their lives important. They had been wrong of course. You don't dream when you are dead. I dream. The living dream, though I won't say thanks for that.

I made my way to the only open bar in the terminal and sat down on a stool that looked as if it had been brought from the factory that night. Everything about the bar and the airport was new and sterile. The tiles on the floor were clean and I saw where minute trails of remaining dust were left in my wake as if to guide me back. I ordered a beer and put my money on the bar. It was light wood lacquered to a mirror shine and I saw my face in the strange piney reflection and scooted my stool back a bit. A janitor swung a mop down the long tile path between the gates, and I took a swallow of my beer and glanced at the fine particles of dust I'd left on the floor in my wake.

"Hey, boss," I said.

He was older, but not old, and he dragged the mop over to me and folded his arms across the end of the pole.

"I hate to bug you, but would you mind if I ran that mop across the floor there." I started to get up to take the mop across the streak I'd left on the floor when I saw him look down.

"Why…there's nothing on that floor, son. Don't worry about it." He reached out to pat my shoulder, but I turned back to the bar and grabbed my beer and finished it. I pointed to the bar and put more dollars on top of the ones the barman had not yet collected.

"I'm sorry. I just thought…," and I must have drifted off because I did not see him move. I saw instead the mop head swaying across the floor in narrow arcs where I'd been pointing. He walked off dragging the dirt gray of the mop's fringes down the concourse behind him.

The bar was polished to a mirror shine and even the windows that looked out onto the runway cast our reflections back on us because of the strange way the yellow light filled the airport. I kept drinking.

"Coming from or going to?" the bartender asked.

"Coming from."

"Which one?"

"Iraq."

"You going back after?"

"Don't think so. Never know," I said.

"Y'all watching your backs over there?"

"Yeah. Doing our best."

"Damn shame, if you ask me."

"What's that?"

"I just hate that y'all have to be over there."

I tipped my beer up to him. "Appreciate that."

"We ought to nuke those sand niggers back to the Stone Age." He started to wipe down the bar. I finished my beer and put five bucks on the bar and asked for another. He set it down in front of me. "Turn the whole place into glass," he said.

I didn't answer.

"Whole place is full of savages, is what I hear."

I looked up at him. He was smiling at me. "Yeah, man. Something like that."

My flight was one of the last of the night. I heard the loudspeaker announce that the Richmond-bound plane was taxiing into place. The pile of money was still on the bar. "I owe for the beers," I said.

He pointed to a yellow ribbon pinned on the wall between a signed eight-by-ten glossy of a daytime soap star and a faded newspaper clipping of a man with a giant catfish splayed over the hood of a red Ford pickup with a rusted front quarter panel.

"What does that mean?"

"On me." He smiled. "It's the least I can do."

"Forget it. I want to pay." I didn't want to smile and say thanks. Didn't want to pretend I'd done anything except survive.

He reached out to shake my hand and I picked up the money and handed it back to him and turned and left.

The pilot made an announcement when all the passengers had taken their seats. Said how honored he was to be giving an American hero a ride home. Fuck it, I thought. I got four free Jack and Cokes out of the deal and a little extra legroom. Then, late in the night, as we flew through a black starless sky above the Eastern Seaboard, as planes carrying other soldiers took off with their noses pointed toward high school friends and eighteen-year-old girls, toward field parties and the banks of streams and ponds, along which young boys would pace out hours in silence after taking the freckled shoulders of those girls into their hands, their hands feeling skin beneath a flip of red or blond or brown hair, and not knowing what to do, those same hands folding as if in prayer, praying without even knowing they are praying, "God, please don't let the world be always slipping from me," and leaving the bright fires and laughter, leaving the rings of cars in fields, passing through the center of the circles that the headlights made, stumbling into the underbrush where they'd feel the balled fist of their loneliness grip some bone inside their chest like it was the slightest and most brittle bone God ever made, after all this, I dropped into a drunken sleep. I dreamed of the wood planks on my mother's porch, the warmth of the sun they held long after sunset, lying there on the warm wood in the cool air thinking only of the sound of the bullfrogs and cicadas on the water, hoping I would dream only of that sound.

And then I was there, simply and without qualification. I sat with my cheeks in my hands out by the smoking area, distracting myself by counting the wads of chewing gum that dotted the concrete, when the sound of a motor approached. I did not raise my eyes. It took her hands on my face to rouse me from my preoccupations.

She pressed hard into the hollows of my cheeks and then stepped back. "Oh, John," she said. Again she advanced and grabbed me hard around my waist. Her hands pushed and rubbed my body. She patted down the front of my uniform and brought her hands back to my face and she pressed down again. I could see that her hands were a little more wrinkled than I recalled, thin bones seen even from the palm side. Had it only been a year? Her grasp was firm, and she touched me hard as if to prove I was not a fleeting apparition. She touched me as though it was the last time she might.

I pulled her hands from my face and held them together out in front of me. "I'm fine, Ma," I said. "Don't make a scene."

She began to cry. She didn't keen or bellow, she just said my name over and over again, "Oh John, oh John, oh John, oh John." When I took her hands from against my cheeks she wrenched one loose and slapped me hard across the mouth and tears welled up in my eyes and I laid my head on her chest. I had to reach down to do it because she was small. She held me there and kept repeating my name, saying, "Oh, John, you're home now."

I don't know how long we stood there like that, with me hunching down to be embraced, but I forgot the sounds of the motor and the people walking past, I forgot the travelers who called out their thanks to me. I was aware of my mother and of her alone. I felt as if I'd somehow been returned to the singular safety of the womb, untouched and untouchable to the world outside her arms around my slouching neck. I was aware of all this, though I am not sure how. Yet when she said, "Oh, John, you're home," I did not believe her.

It wasn't a particularly long ride home in her old Chrysler over the interstate. Half an hour or so. In that time I found myself making strange adjustments to the landscape. We passed over the World War II Veterans Memorial Bridge, which spanned the James, and I stared out at the broad valley below. The sun coming up and a light the color of unripe oranges fell and broke up the mist that hung in the bottom-land.

I pictured myself there. Not as I could be in a few months swimming along the banks beneath the low-slung trunks and branches of walnut and black alder trees, but as I had been. It seemed as if I watched myself patrol through the fields along the river in the yellow light, like I had transposed the happenings of that world onto the contours of this one. I looked for where I might find cover in the field. A slight depression between a narrow dirt track and the water's edge became a rut where a truck must have spun its wheels for a good long while after a rain and I saw that it would grant good cover and concealment from two directions until a base of fire could be laid down which would allow us to fall back.

"You all right, hon?" my mother said. No one was in the field. Certainly I was not. Her voice gave me a start, and I fell back into myself as we reached the other side of the bridge.

"Yeah, Ma, I'm fine."

I let the green blur of trees along highways and side roads lull me into some approximation of comfort until we turned down our gravel driveway. The yard had not been mowed in a long time.

"What's the first thing you want to do, sweetie?" she asked excitedly.

"I'd like to shower and then . . . I don't know, sleep, I guess."

It was almost noon and it was spring and the pond behind the house was quiet. She helped me bring my duffel inside the house, and I went into my room. "I'm putting breakfast on, John, your favorite." Bright sunlight fell between the wood-slatted blinds. I shut them and pulled the curtains over. I shut the light off and pulled the chain dangling from the ceiling fan. The hum of the blades muffled the cars' engines on the street and the soft rattle of pans in the kitchen. I smelled the grease and the unmowed grass. I smelled the clean house and the wood-frame bed. It was all filler. The noise, the sound, they existed just to take up space. My muscles flexed into the emptiness I still called home.

The room was dark and cool. I was tired. I folded my cover and put it on the bedside table. The blouse came off next. Then the belt, hung over the bedpost. I sat on the bed and reached down, unlacing the right boot first, then removing the right sock. In the muddy dimness, the dog tag strung into the laces of my left boot shone. I fingered it and sat upright.

I was disappearing. It was as if I stripped myself away in that darkened bedroom on a spring afternoon, and when I was finished there would be a pile of clothes neatly folded and I would be another number for the cable news shows. I could almost hear it. "Another casualty today," they'd say, "vanished into thin air after arriving home." Fine. I leaned down and finished unlacing the boot and strung the dog tag back around my neck and let it lie against the other. Left boot and left sock off. Pants off. Underwear off. I was gone. I opened the closet door and stood in front of the dressing mirror. My hands and face were tanned to rust. The rest of my body, pale and thinned, hung in the reflection as if of its own accord. I sighed and crawled beneath the cool sheets.

My mind and body waxed and waned under the fan. The sound of motors trilled as they moved toward our house, then lulled off into the distance as they rolled past. A train in the cut beyond the wood line made its shift as well, high-pitched and seeming to hurtle toward my single bed, as if falling toward me, as if I'd become some mass attracting the noise of metal and the metal itself. My pulse fluttered up into my eyes. I exhaled hard whenever the noise rolled past, off toward some other target. I don't remember what I dreamed, but Murph was there, Murph and me and the same ghosts every night. I don't remember what I dreamed, but finally I slept.

6

SEPTEMBER 2004

Al Tafar, Nineveh Province, Iraq

WHEN WE NEARED the orchard a flock of birds lit from its outer rows. They hadn't been there long. The branches shook with their absent weight and the birds circled above in the ruddy mackerel sky, where they made an artless semaphore. I was afraid. I smelled copper and cheap wine. The sun was up, but a half-moon hung low on the opposite horizon, cutting through the morning sky like a figure from a child's pull-tab book.

We were lined along the ditch up to our ankles in a soupy muck. It all seemed in that moment to be the conclusion of a poorly designed experiment in inevitability. Everything was in its proper place, waiting for a pause in time, for the source of all momentum to be stilled, so that what remained would be nothing more than detritus to be tallied up. The world was paper-thin as far as I could tell. And the world was the orchard, and the orchard was what came next. But none of that was true. I was only afraid of dying.

The orchard was quiet. The lieutenant waved his arm from side to side until he had the attention of the sergeants and corporals. When he saw that he did, he made one long sweeping motion in the direction of the orchard and scrambled up out of the ditch. We followed. The only sound was the padding of forty or so boots in the dust, neither running nor walking, and our breathing, which grew louder when we ducked to meet the first low branches and the softness of the orchard floor.

I kept going. I kept going because Murph kept going and Sterling and the LT kept going and the other squads would keep going and I was terrified that I would be the one who did not. So I ducked down under the low-hanging branches and followed the platoon inside.

When the mortars fell, the leaves and fruit and birds were frayed like ends of rope. They lay on the ground in scattered piles, torn feathers and leaves and the rinds of broken fruit intermingling. The sunlight fell absently through the spaces in the treetops, here and there glistening as if on water from smudges of bird blood and citrus.

The squads moved out in an arc, hunched over like old men. We stepped carefully, looking for trip wires or any sign that the enemy was there. No one saw where the fire came from. For a moment it seemed to come from far away through the trees, and I caught myself staring in amazement at the shadows cast by the sunlight falling through the branches. When the first round snapped by my head, I was still thinking that the only shadows I had seen in the war had been made of angles: hard blurs of light falling on masses of buildings, antennas, and the shapes of weapons in tangles of alleys. The bullet came so quickly that the time it took to push that thought out of my head was imperceptible, so that before I even noticed, the other boys were firing back. I began to fire, too, and the noise of the rounds exploding in the chamber pushed in my eardrums and they began to ring and the deafness expanded as if someone had struck a tuning fork at perfect pitch, so that it resonated and wrapped everyone in the orchard in his very own vow of silence.

We didn't see where the fire came from when it came. We saw only the leaves as they flicked about and the small chunks of wood and pieces of earth that danced around us. When the ringing of the first shots subsided, we heard bullets, sounds like small rips in the air, reports of rifles from somewhere we couldn't see. I was struck by a kind of lethargy, in awe of the decisiveness of every single attenuated moment, observed in minute detail each slender moving branch and the narrow bands of sunlight coming through the leaves. Someone pulled me down to the orchard floor, and coming out of it I dragged myself on my elbows behind a withered clump of trees.

Soon there were voices calling out, "Three o'clock, fucking three o'clock!" and though I had not seen anyone to shoot at, I squeezed the trigger, dazzled by the flashes from my muzzle. What looked like an obscene photography began, followed by the shimmer of spent casings as they bounced against the bark.

Again, quiet. Scattered fire teams lay prone all over the beaten earth of the orchard floor. Wide, unblinking eyes exchanged up and down the line became a kind of language. We spoke in whispers, great huffs of breath gone monosyllabic and strangled of volume. We got up, resumed our prior pace.

As we walked on line through the ragged grove, we began to hear a sound from our front. At first it sounded like humbled weeping; closer, a bleating lamb. We moved faster as we were called forward and saw the enemy dead strewn about a shallow ditch: two boys, sixteen or so, their battered rifles lying akimbo at the bottom, had been shot in the face and torso. Their skin had lost most of its natural brown, and I wondered if that was because of the light flickering through the low unkempt canopy or because their blood had congealed in pools at the bottom of the ditch.

The medics had a private from third platoon on the ground, his blouse removed, his teeth chattering, mewling like a lamb. He was gut-shot and dying. We tried to help as much we could, but the medics shoved us back, so we watched and softly said, "Come on, Doc," as they tried to put his insides back in his body. He was a pale shape. The medics were covered in his blood and he shook in his delirium. We stepped away and formed a circle under the light falling through the leaves. His lips turned dark purple in the light and quivered. Snot ran onto his upper lip and the shaking of his body threw small flecks of spittle over his chin. I realized he had been still for a while and he was dead. No one spoke.

"I thought he was going to say something," I finally said.

The rest of the company fanned out. A couple of guys from the other squads in second platoon moved out of the circle. Murph sat with his feet swinging in one of the shallow ditches, cleaning his rifle. A few acknowledged that they'd been waiting for him to say something, too. When he only died, their faces became downcast and surprised. They moved aimlessly away.

Sterling stubbed out a cigarette near the boy's body with his toe and a thin rail of smoke rose toward the tattered leaves and dissipated. "They usually don't," he said. "I only heard it once."

An embedded photographer snapped pictures of it all: a private snaking his barrel in a ditch, the dead boy, as yet uncovered, gazing thinly toward the blue sky that had cleared itself of clouds high above the orchard. I thought that he had no regard for the significance of what he saw. But now I think maybe he did. Maybe his regard was absolute.

"What did he say?" I asked.

"Who?" Sterling said.

"The KIA. What did he say?"

"Nothing really. I was holding his hand. Freaked the fuck out, you know? Fire was still coming in. I was the only one there. Doesn't matter." He paused. "I didn't even know the guy." Sterling grabbed at the collar of his vest and closed his eyes and breathed in deeply. He nodded to the photographer and they began to pick their way through the debris; the branches and torn rinds, the dead and the living.

"What did he say?" I asked again.

He turned back. "Bart, you're just gonna make it into something bigger than it was. You ought to go check your boy and quit worrying about that shit."

I turned and saw Murph kneeling next to the body. His hands were on his thighs. I could have gone to Murph, but I did not. I didn't want to. I didn't want to be responsible for him. I had enough to worry about. I was disintegrating, too. How was I supposed to keep us both intact?

It is possible that I broke my promise in that very moment, that if I'd gone to comfort him a second earlier, he might not have broken himself. I don't know. He didn't look distraught, he looked curious. He touched the body, straightened the collar, put the boy's head in his lap.

I had to know. "C'mon, Sarge. Just tell me." He looked at me. I could see that he was as tired as I was. That surprised me.

"Well, he was crying," said Sterling. "And he was all like, 'I'm fucking dying, right?' And I was like, 'Yeah, probably.' And he kept crying harder and then he stopped and I was just waiting for him to keep talking, or whatever. You know, like in the movies or some shit."

"Well?"

"He goes, 'Hey, man, check if I shat my pants.' Then he was dead." Sterling clapped his hands together as if to signal that he was done with it, had struck it from his mind.

I turned away, overwhelmed and dizzy, and vomited until I had nothing left in me. But still the bile came out in sickly yellow ribbons. I rose from my stomach to my knees and I wiped it from my mouth. "What the fuck, man? What the fuck?" is all I could think to say as I spit into the ditch, then turned and walked away to the sound of a shutter clicking.

A few hours later we linked up with the rest of the company. The reserve platoon secured a perimeter. We were supposed to sleep. The day was not over for us. Murph and I found a hole and tried to nod off but couldn't.

"You know what, Bart?" Murph said.

"What?"

"I cut in front of that kid in line at the DFAC."

I looked around. "What kid?"

"The dead kid."

"Oh," I said. "It's cool, man. Don't sweat it."

"I feel like a dick."

"It's all right."

"I feel fucking crazy right now." He had his head in his hands. He kept rubbing his eyes with the base of his palms. "I was really happy it wasn't me. That's crazy, right?"

"Naw. You know what's crazy? Not thinking that shit."

I had thought the same thing, how glad I was not to be

shot, how much it would have hurt to be there dying, watching all of us watch him die. And I too, though sad now, had said to myself, Thank God he died and I did not. Thank you, God.

I tried to cheer him up. "Got to be at least nine eighty, right?"

"Yeah. Something like that," he said.

It didn't work. It was a shitty little war.

We moved on. A lark or finch called as I planted my tired footsteps into the dust. I looked over my shoulder and reinforced that I had been and was still going. My footsteps marked my passage. I made more, more firmly planted in accordance with my training. I held my rifle in accordance with my training. Through this I gained strength and purpose. I have leafed through heavy manuals and have found only these things to be certain in accordance with my training.

The empty city smoldered. We wore it to the bone with our modern instruments. Walls crumbled. Blocks composed of halves of shelled buildings allowed warm breezes to sweep up trash and dust and send them swirling in little cyclones as we walked. We took breaks for water, smoked where we pleased, reclined in chairs behind unoccupied desks. Empty shops with wood-fronted booths still stocked with wares from times at once ancient and obscure filled the bazaars. We placed our feet on the desks, as the soles of our boots could not offend the dead.

We walked in alleys. Saw the remnants of the enemy where they lay in ambush, pushed them off their weapons with our boots. Rigid and pestilent, the bodies lay bloating in the sun. Some lay at odd angles with backs curved slightly off the ground and others were wrenched at absurd degrees, their decay an echo of some morbid geometry.

We walked through the city, down pockmarked valleys of concrete and brick that bore the weight of old cars burning, seeming to follow the destruction as it spread rather than spreading it ourselves. No one around but an old woman. I caught glimpses of her, briefly, a shuffling gait as she floated out of sight. As we turned corners she was turning opposite and I had no solid picture but her form receding, shawled in an old quilt that gave her shapeless comfort.

We stopped at a corner. A parade of rats crossed the street, weaving through the detritus. By force of numbers they shooed a mangy dog away from the corpse that it fed upon. I watched the dog as it loped off down an alley with a mangled arm clenched tightly in its jaws. Soon the dog was out of sight and the lieutenant raised his hand to signal to the platoon to stop near a bridge that crossed over the Tigris and the sparsely wooded banks below. A spare quiet and the river flowing softly nearby. A body sprawled in the center of the bridge. His head was cut off and it lay on his chest like some perverted Russian doll.

"Oh fuck," the lieutenant whispered.

Someone asked him what was going on. I could see on his

face, as he peered through his binoculars, the unmistakable look of recognition.

"Body bomb," he said. All stopped. It was impossible to know who the man was or what brought him to that place, and it was hard to fathom because a moment is never long enough to account for tragedy when you are in it. Grief is a practical mechanism, and we only grieved those we knew. All others who died in Al Tafar were part of the landscape, as if something had sown seeds in that city that made bodies rise from the earth, in the dirt or up through the pavement like flowers after a frost, dried and withering under a cold, bright sun.

An interminable silence passed. As a group we were on a knee, looking out at the body, wondering what should be done. The lieutenant stood and turned to us, but before he could utter a word we were overtaken by blindness, as if the sun had fallen out of the sky. We were covered in dust and deafened before any sound could reach us. I lay groggy on the ground and my ears rang and buzzed loudly and as I looked up I saw the rest of the platoon moving on the ground, trying to get their bearings. Sterling was covered in black dust. His mouth moved and he gestured to his rifle, pointed out what he saw and began to fire at it. In alleys beneath us, closer to the riverbank, and in windows above us, we saw the tips of rifles and hands. The buzz in my head was oppressive, and I couldn't hear the bullets as they passed, but I felt a few as they cut the air. The fight was hazy and without sound, as if it was happening under-water.

I moved to the edge of the bridge and began firing at any-thing moving. I saw one man fall in a heap near the bank of the river among the bulrushes and green fields on its edges. In that moment, I disowned the waters of my youth. My memories of them became a useless luxury, their names as foreign as any that could be found in Nineveh: the Tigris or the Chesapeake, the James or the Shatt al Arab farther to the south, all belonged to someone else, and perhaps had never really been my own. I was an intruder, at best a visitor, and would be even in my home, in my misremembered his-tory, until the glow of phosphorescence in the Chesapeake I had longed to swim inside again someday became a taunt against my insignificance, a cruel trick of light that had al-ways made me think of stars. No more. I gave up longing, because I was sure that anything seen at such a scale would reveal the universe as cast aside and drowned, and if I ever floated there again, out where the level of the water reached my neck, and my feet lost contact with its muddy bottom, I might realize that to understand the world, one's place in it, is to be always at the risk of drowning.

Noctiluca, I thought, *Ceratium,* as the tracers began to show themselves in sifted twilight, two words learned on a school field trip to the tidewaters of Virginia that appeared as I was shooting at the man, paying no attention then to the strange connections made inside of any mind, the small storms of electricity that cause them to rise and then submerge, then rise again. A fleeting thought of a young girl sitting beside me on a dock, back there the twilight coming on, the crack of tracers as I shot and shot again, the man crawling from his weapon until he stopped and his blood trickled down into the river in its final ebbing tide, brief as bioluminescence. Sterling and Murph came over and sat next to me and we took out more magazines and fired those into his body and his clothes were awash in blood and it ran down the low bank and flowed into the river until it all had been exhausted.

"Now you've got it, Privates. Thorough, thorough is the way home."

I stopped firing and put my head in my hands. My rifle slung in my lap. I had taken it as far as I could. I looked over at Sterling. His face was serene. I wondered what he could do beyond this. No, what could I do beyond this? Where would he take us?

We regrouped. A head count revealed no casualties except for a few broken eardrums from the blast. We returned to the spot where we had been previously and waited for the QRF. There was a wet spot where the body had been and its remnants were scattered in pieces, some small and some large, others appearing infinite like the pieces we found near our feet: a piece of skin and muscle, entrails. Others were larger, an arm and bits of legs closer to where he'd been. No one said a word but in the silence we re-created the last few moments of his life in our minds. We saw him struggling and begging and asking Allah to free him, then realizing he would not be saved as they cut his throat and his neck bled and he choked and died.

The man had been made an unwilling weapon. They'd captured and killed him and eviscerated him and stuffed his abdominal cavity with explosives, detonated him when they were sure we had recognized him, then attacked. As the QRF arrived, we were told that the bridge had to be cleared.

Sterling called out, "Murph, Bartle!"

We took grappling hooks and tried to snag the larger pieces of the body. We yanked on them until we were sure they were free of explosives and posed no further threat. Murph threw the metal implement from behind a low wall and pulled until the chunks of the body resisted, then jerked hard on the rope. He looked at me when he had tugged hard on his piece, and then it was my turn. After we repeated the process several times, an officer got out of his vehicle and declared the bridge cleared.

As we continued through the city, people began returning in twos and threes and set about the task of burying the dead. I heard the muezzin call and the sun went down purple and red, painting the city softly.

7

AUGUST 2005

Richmond, Virginia

THAT SPRING WHOLE days and weeks were slept through and swept into the afternoons, never seeing a soul. I woke at random intervals to hear the school bus down the street loading and unloading different grades and ages of children, telling me the time based on the pitch of their chattering voices.

I had deteriorated more than one might expect in the short time I'd been home. My only exercise was the two-mile round trip I made every afternoon to G.W.'s country store for a case of beer. I avoided roads, opting instead for the train tracks that passed by our house on the other side of a long, low berm. The hardwoods canopied above me provided shade, and the light fell through the green branches unceremoniously. The heat had gathered throughout the spring and now became a dense murk in the trellised pathway of the train tracks. Atlantic heat: muggy, thick with mosquitoes. It was quite unlike the heat in Al Tafar, which had the surprising effect of reducing one to tears in an instant, even after having spent hours broiling in it already. This heat was somehow more American; it confronted you immediately on your stepping out in it. Your breath warmed intolerably and it seemed you needed to push through it like a swimmer.

Sometimes, when I reached G.W.'s, I'd wait just inside the wood line until whatever old pickup turned its last rusted quarter panel down the road, and I'd walk into the chime of the double doors through the dust it had left in its wake. I can't really explain what that feeling was like. Shame, I guess. But that wasn't all of it. It was more particular than that. Anyone can feel shame. I remember myself, sitting in the dirt under neglected and overgrown brush, afraid of nothing in the world more than having to show myself for what I had become. I wasn't really known around there anyway, but I had the feeling that if I encountered anyone they would intuit my disgrace and would judge me instantly. Nothing is more isolating than having a particular history. At least that's what I thought. Now I know: All pain is the same. Only the details are different.

When I got back to the house, my shirt soaked through with sweat and starched again with salt, I'd put the beer in my closet, and walk into the kitchen, where I'd stand for a long time looking out the window onto the haze rising off the pond. I didn't want to broaden the evidence of my existence wider than brief footprints of moisture on the floor of my mother's modest country kitchen. I looked out the window and saw the street and railroad tracks, the woods beyond. Beyond the woods, the county of which they were a part. And so on, until it all dissolved into the larger thing: my mother's house becoming every other house as I once had seen it, sitting atop the southern end of a broad river valley, close enough to the mountains that every few years a scared black bear would wander down into the remaining forest, and close enough to the ocean that those early English settlers took it as the farthest point they'd go upstream, the geology of the place preventing them from having any choice other than the one wherein they said, "We are lost; therefore we will call this home." And close enough that as a child I had been teased by older kids who said if I only tried hard enough I would smell salt water, and I, believing, stood among the light poles and the gulls in the parking lots of A&Ps and cried when I knew that it was true despite the fact that they had meant to lie, as children sometimes do.

The house itself rested above one of many ponds and streams meandering down to the James like so many pieces of unwound rope. And on the other side: Richmond, its glass buildings sometimes reflecting the river below, or clouds, or ironworks and track nearly gone to powder with rust. There it sat, up on its escarpment, which the river had scoured out over the millennia, and still it dug farther into the earth, winding in the landscape like a salesman's banner unfurling to reveal his wares.

Back home, everything had begun to remind me of something else. Every thought I had blossomed outward and backward until it attached itself to some other memory, that one leading to another, impermanent, until I was lost to whatever present moment I was in. "Honey, do you mind fixing the fence out by the pond?" my mother would say in the shortening days of summer, and I would walk into the long expanse of the yard holding a hammer and a fistful of nails and I'd reach the fence and lean on it, looking out over the water as warm breezes made it ripple and I'd be brought back. Back to what? To nothing, to everything. The yelp of dogs echoing out from where they rolled in wet garbage in the shadow of the Shamash Gate. If I heard the caw of ugly crows swing down from the power line that they adorned in black simplicity, the caws might strike in perfect harmony with the memory of the sound of falling mortars, and I, at home now, might brace for the impact, come on, you motherfuckers, I'd think, you finally got me, and then as the birds took flight I would remember and I'd look back and see my mother's face silhouetted in the kitchen window and I'd smile back at her and wave, take the loosening wire meshing of the fence and begin to nail it back in place. You want to fall, that's all. You think it can't go on like that. It's as if your life is a perch on the edge of a cliff and going forward seems impossible, not for a lack of will, but a lack of space. The possibility of another day stands in defiance of the laws of physics. And you can't go back. So you want to fall, let go, give up, but you can't. And every breath you take reminds you of that fact. So it goes.

Late August. I left my mother's house. I'd developed the habit of taking long, aimless walks to fill the days. I woke one morning in a small room off the kitchen in my single bed wishing that I hadn't. It wasn't the first time. I was tired of my mind running all night through the things I remembered, then through things I did not remember but for which I blamed myself on account of the sheer vividness of scenes that looped on the red-green linings of my closed eyelids. I could not tell what was true and what I had invented but I wanted it to stop, to leave it and have my perception drift away like a burned-up fog. I wanted to go to sleep and stay there, that's all. A passive wish, one I didn't push. Sure, there is a fine line between not wanting to wake up and actually wanting to kill yourself, and while I discovered you can walk that line for a long while without even noticing, anybody who is around you surely will, and then of course all kinds of unanswerable questions will not be far behind.

The phone rang one morning. Ma picked it up. "It's Luke, honey," she said, calling to me from the other room. Eleven o'clock. Still in bed.

"Tell him I'll call him back."

She walked into my room and put the mouthpiece to her chest. "You've got to talk to people, John. It's not good to be by yourself so much."

I'd known Luke since middle school. He was my best friend, though even now, those words don't seem to mean anything. My fault, not his. His name reminded me of that discovery you make as a kid, that if you say a word over and over it will start to sound like gibberish, like white noise. "Take a message," I said.

She looked at me.

"I'll call him back, Ma. Promise."

She put the phone up to her ear and turned away. "He's tired, Luke. Can he call you back? ... Tomorrow? All right. I'll tell him."

"We done?" I asked.

"Goddammit, Johnny," she huffed. "They're going to the river tomorrow afternoon. They want to see you. People want to see you."

"All right."

"All right, what?"

"All right, maybe."

"You'll think about it?"

"Yeah."

"I really think you should. Just think about it." She smiled tentatively.

"Goddammit, Mama. All I fucking do is think."

I put my pants on and I went out onto the back porch and spit over the handrail, and it was a yellowish brown, and my body pulsed with a warm obtuse ache from my eyelids to my fingertips. The ache was inside my body too, an all-encompassing type of pain like my whole skin was made out of a fat lip. I lit a cigarette and went down to the pond behind her house, the light all bright and shimmery like raw linen in the dense summer air, then farther back into the woods where the pond drained into a creek and ran between steeply gouged-out red-clay banks. At a spot where the creek caught up and swirled and eddied between exposed rocks, I found a place I'd often come to as a child. A large boulder overhung the creek, the red clay long since weathered away. Roots of a large gray birch clung to the side of the rock and went down into the ground where it leveled off into a clearing next to the creek. The leaves in the canopies of central Virginia's hardwood forests had begun their pre-autumnal yellow tightening and they hung over the clearing and the creek and the light fell through them in a way that I was fond of and the morning was kind of soft-edged and clumsy like I'd been seeing it through gauze.

I made my way down the steep clay bank and tottered along a downed tree that crossed the creek. The rocks were slick but they were not as far apart as I remembered, and it was not too hard to get across because the previous night's beers had me moving at a deliberate pace. I used my hands to brace myself as I made my way beneath the overhang, and though the morning had already begun to warm up it was cool under there, and I could feel the cool from the moisture of the big rock against my hands. Up on a birch, the initials J.B. had been carved into the sheet of silver bark a half-dozen times, each one a slightly different size from the others, with various patterns of lines where the cuts had stretched out with the tree's growth. I climbed over to the tree and rubbed my fingers, all dull and warm, into the cut marks. I could not remember making the marks, but I was sure I'd made them. Of course J.B. is not an uncommon pair of initials, but I was sure I'd made the carvings and I could not remember anything about doing them and so I smiled.

I sat down there awhile until the sun was straight above me and the light fell down in wide columns and sweat ran down between my shoulder blades. I decided then to walk the tracks toward the city. It wasn't so much a decision as it was a product of trying to turn off my mind. I couldn't stop thinking about Murph. I drifted and followed the guidance of the tops of my boots and I tried not to think and when I got back up to the porch, I wiped the sweat from my forehead, opened the sliding door, put a few things in my duffel bag, and left.

I hadn't known what I was doing then, but my memories of Murph were a kind of misguided archaeology. Sifting through the remains of what I remembered about him was a denial of the fact that a hole was really all that was left, an absence I had attempted to reverse but found that I could not. There was simply not enough material to account for what had been removed. The closer I got to reconstructing him in my mind, the more the picture I was trying to re-create receded. For every memory I was able to pull up, another seemed to fall away forever. There was some proportion about it all, though. It was like putting a puzzle together from behind: the shapes familiar, the picture quickly fading, the muted tan of the cardboard backing a tease at wholeness and completion. I'd think of a time when we sat in the evening in the guard tower, watching the war go by in streaks of red and green and other, briefer lights, and he'd tell me of an afternoon in the little hillside apple orchard that his mother worked, the turn and flash of a paring knife along a wrap of gauze as they grafted uppers to rootstocks and new branches to blossom, or the time he saw but could not explain his awe when his father brought a dozen caged canaries home from the mine and let them loose in the hollow where they lived, how the canaries only flitted and sang awhile before perching back atop their cages, which had been arranged in rows, his father likely thinking that the birds would not return by choice to their captivity, and that the cages should be used for something else: a pretty bed for vegetables, perhaps a place to string up candles between the trees, and in what strange silences the world worked, Murph must have wondered, as the birds settled peaceably in their formation and ceased to sing. And I'd try to recall things until nothing came, which I quickly found was my only certainty, until what was left of him was a sketch in shadow, a skeleton falling apart, and my friend Murph was no more friend to me than the strangest stranger. My missing him became a grave that could not be filled or leveled, just a faded blemish in a field and a damn poor substitute for grief, as graves so often are.

So I took the railroad tracks, roughly following the old Danville line northeast toward the city. It began to rain a little. The creosote seeped out of the railroad ties and became slick, and the wet gray aggregate shifted under my boots. I walked slowly, more or less shuffling from one railroad tie to the next, hardly looking up. Though I was in no hurry and had no destination in mind, the trees opened up and before I realized how far I'd gone I was above the river standing on the railroad bridge's first trestled arch. The sun would soon be going down behind the trees, and the river was calm and flat, and it bent out of sight and trailed gently off toward its beginning in the mountains. The water was all a bright purple and orange where it reflected the ruddy clouds in the fading light, and I looked over the railing down onto the old stone piers of earlier iterations of the bridge where earlier iterations of aimless walkers must have seen some kind of sight like this and stopped and stood for a while and looked out over the water taking a deep breath and maybe seeing a small wavy outline of themselves reflected down below, with all that space around, thinking there was just so much damn space to be in that it hurt.

Soon enough I felt the dull rumble of a train shudder up the tracks, and I saw the first hint of its lamplight coming around the bend on the river's other side. The sun was not quite down yet so the light around the bend was indistinct and only twinkling a little, like a star seen at daybreak or dusk. I slid down off the trestle and a little ways down the steep dirt bank and then I sat and watched the outline of the train moving, skylit, over the bridge from one side to the other. I could barely make out windows, much less see into them, so I did not see if the train was crowded but still I thought I might want to be on it. Maybe the train was coming from D.C., crossing the bridge north to south as it was. Maybe it was headed down to Raleigh or Asheville or perhaps cutting west on a hitch line out toward Roanoke and the Blue Ridge. I looked for a place to jump on but I did not see one because the train against the sky and the lights of the city to the east moved like a black shape in the blacker night.

A small deer run led down the hill below the bridgehead toward the flat, muddy riverbanks. There were fifty yards or so of good bottomland with birches and elms scattered around and then little islands leading farther out which became sparse until they were just spits of sand and muck between dark runnels of water. The broad river, not yet whitecapped, ran a half or a quarter of a mile to the other bank. Beyond the river and up the opposite hill, the city stood outlined against the sky. It squatted on the high ground above yet more rail lines and past the remains of a canal carved out by colonial merchants who sought to break the impediment of the fall line which Richmond straddled. And it seemed, as I lit a fire by the waterside and sat under a lean-to of birch branches, that whole rotations had reversed themselves and that I alone watched the city and the ground on which it sat spin throughout the night inside the universe.

When I woke I saw that the fire had decayed to ember in the night. It was late morning and the sand in the bright light looked like burlap sacking where I'd slept. The driftwood from the fire was all black and charred. Music swam toward me from a boom box leveled on a midstream rock where a group of boys and girls about my age lay out on towels or jumped into the swift water, laughing. I could see Luke, but I couldn't tell who the others were.

The ash and smoke had seeped into my skin while the fire burned out during the night, and I waded into the water below the rail bridge to try to wash it off, but I could still smell it an hour later. I climbed back up the hill and onto the tracks again and shuffled across the bridge one hundred feet above the water. I moved to the edge where the ties met the structure of the bridge itself and moved along the oxidized metal, occasionally swinging my foot out over the water flowing down below while watching the kids laugh and swim in the fresh water. The day was warm and clear, and the sky behind the city was bright blue and empty. When I got to the north bank of the river, I followed the tracks toward the city for a while, then turned down a worn path that led toward the water.

It was hard to cross the canal and even though it had been cut out some two hundred years before, it still seemed industrial and slightly dirty. Finally, I found a spot where the river hung up behind a couple of downed oaks on the canal side and doubled back toward the path along the river's edge. It took me to a campsite looking right out over the water, and it was the afternoon now and the site was empty but only recently so. Three lean-tos perched beneath strong, firm elms bordered a small clearing with a fire pit and a few stumps for seating.

I set my duffel on the ground and got a fire going and took my boots off and my clothes off and hung them on a branch near the fire. My feet were in the water, and the river ran docilely by and I was hardly a speck on the landscape and I was glad. An egret flew just over my shoulder and skimmed the water so close and I thought there was no way a body could be so close to the edge of a thing and stay there and be in control. But the tips of its wings skimmed along the water just the same. The egret didn't seem to mind what I believed, and it tilted some and disappeared into the glare of the gone sun and it was full of grace.

Small lines wound their way up and down the surface of the stump on which I sat. They were intricate and sort of gouged out or termited into a pattern that struck me as oddly orderly. Luke and the rest of the boys and girls still splashed in the water, taking turns diving from the broad gray rocks into a little draft of current that swept them ten or twenty feet downstream like an amusement park ride. They were beautiful. I had to resist the urge to hate them.

I had become a kind of cripple. They were my friends,

right? Why didn't I just wade out to them? What would I say? "Hey, how are you?" they'd say. And I'd answer, "I feel like I'm being eaten from the inside out and I can't tell anyone what's going on because everyone is so grateful to me all the time and I'll feel like I'm ungrateful or something. Or like I'll give away that I don't deserve anyone's gratitude and really they should all hate me for what I've done but everyone loves me for it and it's driving me crazy." Right.

Or should I have said that I wanted to die, not in the sense of wanting to throw myself off of that train bridge over there, but more like wanting to be asleep forever because there isn't any making up for killing women or even watching women get killed, or for that matter killing men and shooting them in the back and shooting them more times than necessary to actually kill them and it was like just trying to kill everything you saw sometimes because it felt like there was acid seeping down into your soul and then your soul is gone and knowing from being taught your whole life that there is no making up for what you are doing, you're taught that your whole life, but then even your mother is so happy and proud because you lined up your sight posts and made people crumple and they were not getting up ever and yeah they might have been trying to kill you too, so you say, What are you gonna do?, but really it doesn't matter because by the end you failed at the one good thing you could have done, the one person you promised would live is dead, and you have seen all things die in more manners than you'd like to recall and for a while the whole thing fucking ravaged your spirit like some deep-down shit, man, that you didn't even realize you had until only the animals made you sad, the husks of dogs filled with explosives and old arty shells and the fucking guts and everything stinking like metal and burning garbage and you walk around and the smell is deep down into you now and you say, How can metal be so on fire? and Where is all this fucking trash coming from? and even back home you're getting whiffs of it and then that thing you started to notice slipping away is gone and now it's becoming inverted, like you have bottomed out in your spirit but yet a deeper hole is being dug because everybody is so fucking happy to see you, the murderer, the fucking accomplice, the at-bare-minimum bearer of some fucking responsibility, and everyone wants to slap you on the back and you start to want to burn the whole goddamn country down, you want to burn every goddamn yellow ribbon in sight, and you can't explain it but it's just, like, Fuck you, but then you signed up to go so it's all your fault, really, because you went on purpose, so you are in the end doubly fucked, so why not just find a spot and curl up and die and let's make it as painless as possible because you are a coward and, really, cowardice got you into this mess because you wanted to be a man and people made fun of you and pushed you around in the cafeteria and the hallways in high school because you liked to read books and poems sometimes and they'd call you fag and really deep down you know you went because you wanted to be a man and that's never gonna happen now and you're too much of a coward to be a man and get it over with so why not find a clean, dry place and wait it out with it hurting as little as possible and just wait to go to sleep and not wake up and fuck 'em all.

I started crying. Through my tears night had fallen. The girls in the hot summer night were toweling off and laughing, standing on the darkening rocks beneath the soft light of the lampposts on the nearby train bridge. I got up and followed a path that skirted the banks of the river and I followed it aimlessly. At the edge of the river, I waded in. It was hot then, but the river cooled me, and the moon above the trees on the hilltop, blocking the streetlights, kept the river flickering softly, and I felt myself calmly fading in it. As I leaned forward and floated, I drifted a little, a little down, a little to sleep.

The river had a dream in it. I faced the opposite bank and stood there naked in the water. I saw a band of horses in a field dotted with dogwood and willow. Each was like the others in temperament, all roans except for a single old palomino that looked at me as the others grazed in the thin moonlight. It was bloodied on its hooves and carried the marks of both lash and brand on its haunches. Ducking its head sweetly, it entered the shallow water. As it walked toward me the blood washed downstream and the horse left a little red wake as it walked. It stepped lightly, but bore no grimace on its face, and was only tentative in its step. I stood, still naked, and softly splashed the water around me with both hands. Not hard, just back and forth through the water with my hands in semicircles. It neared and I watched it snort a little and as it neared it shook its head, once, twice, calmly. It stood before me, old and worn from the lash and it bled into the gently flowing water and stood tall despite its wounds. It leaned in and nuzzled me about my shoulder and neck and I leaned in too and nuzzled back and put my arms around it and I could feel the power in its bruised old muscles. The horse's eyes were black and soft.

This was my vision as I woke. Goddamn the noise. The yelling closed in. Them yelling, "Get him out. Goddamn it, get his ass out." I shocked awake and spat up water from the river and they banged on my chest until I spat out more and I lay on the bank, drunk and smiling, looking out at the strange faces gathered there. I lay for a little while half in and out of the water and it ran over my feet, lapping up and down and cooling them, shallow enough to be safe where I lay. I smiled absently and thought of the old palomino nuzzling me as I came around. Whatever. They called me in the lamplight. Night now.

Luke had seen me floating and called 911 from one of the girls' cells. The cops didn't make me go through the motions of any kind of psych evaluation out of respect for my service. I'd given them my military ID when they asked for one and they said, "All right, soldier. Let's get you home." When they dropped me off at my house one of the cops looked at me with a pitiable concern and said, "Try to keep it together, buddy. You'll be back in the swing in no time."

When I opened the door my mother was waiting. She

grabbed at my face and began kissing my cheeks and fore-head. "I thought I'd lost you." she said.

"I'm fine, Momma. Everything is fine."

"I don't understand what's happening to you. I've been worried half to death." She stood there, then moved to the counter and started shuffling the letters nervously where they were stacked. "You know I'm getting calls now too, on top of this," she said.

"Yeah? Who from?"

She turned to look at me and I saw in her eyes all the pain and horror that I had given her. "Some captain. He said he was from the C.I.D." She mouthed the words slowly. "The Criminal Investigation Division. He wants to talk to you." She paused and moved toward me again. I moved away and went into my room and closed the door. Her voice came through the cheap layers of artificial wood. "What happened over there, Johnny? What happened, baby? What did you do?"

What happened? What fucking happened? That's not even the question, I thought. How is that the question? How do you answer the unanswerable? To say what happened, the mere facts, the disposition of events in time, would come to seem like a kind of treachery. The dominoes of moments, lined up symmetrically, then tumbling backward against the hazy and unsure push of cause, showed only that a fall is every object's destiny. It is not enough to say what happened. Everything happened. Everything fell.

8

OCTOBER 2004

Al Tafar, Nineveh Province, Iraq

FALL CAME AT the tail end of our first storm. We'd been granted a reprieve from the heat and the dust, both gently smothered by flat sheets of rain fallen from skies the color of unworked iron. We were still tense, but now we were tense *and* wet.

On a morning several days after the fight in the orchard a major came to our platoon area just before first light. Our platoon had done well in the orchard, minimized civilian casualties, killed a lot of hajjis and suffered only a few casualties of our own. This had earned us good duty: regular patrols with forty-eight hours on and twenty-four off. When the major arrived, we were just returning from one of our cushier patrols through the sparsely occupied buildings on the southern outskirts of Al Tafar. We casually tossed our equipment on the ground and lolled against the low concrete barriers and trees in whatever position was easiest to achieve.

"Platoon, ah-ten-shun!" barked the major's aide as they sauntered into our area through a veil of camo netting.

The LT was snoring, stretched out on top of a concrete enclosure where we'd often wait out mortar barrages, playing spades or engaging in close-quarter wrestling matches until the last bits of shrapnel whistled by. He didn't move. The major and his aide looked at each other, then at us, and we looked back at them only slightly more aware of their presence than we'd been the moment before. Even Sterling remained unstirred. All his gear was on, as taut and orderly as ever, but we'd spent the three hours prior to dawn waiting for a medevac that couldn't fly through the cloud cover from the storm, carefully picking thin slivers of metal out of a boy's face and neck while we huddled in a sewage ditch. We were tired.

The aide cleared his throat. "Ah-ten-shun!" he said, louder this time, but we enjoyed resting in the cool rain and the quiet of the early hour and hardly noticed.

Sterling roused himself, looked over at the LT sleeping soundly, and said, "At ease," with what little earnestness he could muster.

We began to mill about as the major spoke. Only Sterling kept his military bearing and remained attentive. I think it was all that he had left at that point. On the periphery of our gentle domestic activities, citations were read. All the while, weapons were cleaned on dry squares of ground below camouflage nets and tarps, other boys ignored the rain and washed the dust and salt out of their clothes in red plastic buckets full of water gone brown and dingy with their filth, and still others traded care package items for packs of smokes, lighting up and coalescing into the major's audience. But most paid the unasked-for ceremony the attention they thought that it was worth, and as the major spoke, the orders bestowing medals of gallantry and commendation upon us became soaked through, falling apart into wet organic tatters, whereupon they were received from him or not as each name was called, depending on the interest level of the boy in question at the time.

Only Sterling's promotion caused any comment, and most of that because it was accompanied by a Bronze Star for valor. But we said, "Good job, Sarge" and "You earned it, Sarge," and took turns patting him on the back. He gave the major a crisp salute, a sharp about-face, and sat back down against his tree trunk, the ribboned medal hidden in his palm.

After the major and his aide disappeared I noticed that Murph had missed the ceremony. Over the next few weeks I started to get the impression he was avoiding me. There wasn't any particular thing that made me curious at first. He was aloof on patrol, which happened from time to time. When I saw him on the FOB, he would act as if he were in a hurry, or he'd turn his back to me when I tried to catch up to me, casting down his eyes when we'd make contact. But you give a guy a break at times like those. Shit, it wasn't but a year or so since he'd spent the better part of his life buried in that goddamn mine he was always talking about. "Shipp Mountain," he'd say, "now that's a bitch. We'd go down in, three, four o'clock in the morning, laying on this cart and I'd just lay back and look up and think the whole world's a couple feet above me, just looking for a seam to let loose and bust me into nothing. Damn, Bart," he'd say, "I don't recall seeing the sun for weeks at a time."

"No shit?"

"Honest and true," he'd say.

It was heating up in Al Tafar then, and we'd be out on patrol hour after hour, so hot that it seemed that the dust gave off its own light even after the sun went down, so fucking hot that we'd joke with Sterling to get a rise out of him. "Sarge, it's a hundred and twenty degrees. Why don't we surrender and go home," one of us would say.

"Shut your fucking cock holsters," he'd answer if he was in a bad mood. Those rare days he could be said to have been in something resembling a good mood, he'd look back at us as we struggled over a wall or tried to scramble up over the scree of a sewage ditch, and he'd smile and say, "Life is pain." And I'd tell Murph, both of us blinded by a sun that seemed at times to be the whole sky, "It would have been nice if somebody could have eased us into this shit."

I spent a lot of time trying to identify the exact point at which I noticed a change in Murph, somehow thinking that if I could figure out where he had begun to slide down the curve of the bell that I could do something about it. But these are subtle shifts, and trying to distinguish them is like trying to measure the degrees of gray when evening comes. It's impossible to identify the cause of anything, and I began to see the war as a big joke, for how cruel it was, for how desperately I wanted to measure the particulars of Murph's new, strange behavior and trace it back to one moment, to one cause, to one thing I would not be guilty of. And I realized very suddenly one afternoon while throwing rocks into a bucket in a daze that the joke was in fact on me. Because how can you measure deviation if you don't know the mean? There was no center in the world. The curves of all our bells were cracked.

I couldn't think of anything else. My days passed sitting in the dust, throwing rocks into a bucket, missing, didn't matter. I thought a lot about that ridiculous promise I'd made to Murphy's mother. I couldn't even remember what I'd said, or even what had been asked for. Bring him home? What, in one piece? At all? I couldn't remember. Would I have failed if he wasn't happy, if he was no longer sane? How the hell could I protect that which I couldn't see, even in myself? Fuck you, bitch, I'd think, and then think it all again.

I finally went to Sterling with my concerns. He laughed. "Some people just can't fucking hack it, Private. You'd better get used to the fact that Murph's a dead man."

I scoffed. "No way, Sarge. Murph's got his shit together."

And I tried to laugh off Sterling's comment, turning back to him. "Nothing's gonna happen to Murph, he's solid."

Sterling sat carving reliefs of animals into a broken ax handle beneath the slight cover of tree branches. "Private, you forget the edge you've got, because the edge is normal now." He paused and lit a cigarette. It dangled out of his mouth and the ash grew long as he returned to his whittling. "If you get back to the States in your head before your ass is there too, then you are a fucking dead man. I'm telling you. You don't know where Murph keeps going, but I do."

"Where is that, Sarge?" I asked.

"Murph is home, Bartle. And he's gonna be there with a flag shoved up his ass before you know it."

I walked off, intending to look for Murph, when Sterling called after me. "There's only one way home for real, Private. You've got to stay deviant in this motherfucker."

In a way, I knew it was true. Over the next few days Murph came to embody an opacity I couldn't penetrate further. I had my own speculations. On our days off I gave myself free rein to explore them. I talked to myself in bunkers at the few rarely traveled edges of our FOB, fueled by cheap Jordanian whiskey. My mutterings in the dark were punctuated by short percussive sobs. I was becoming spectral, too. An afterthought. I began to visualize my own death in those raw, purposeless tubes of concrete between which I wandered in the evenings. If someone could have seen me, if I could have been seen, then I might have looked like I'd been hurtled into my future, huddling under roofs of an urban landscape just below street level. My mutterings would not seem uncharacteristic, but rather inevitable, and the passing men and women would not pay me much attention. They might in their passing talk say, "What a shame he couldn't get it back together." And one might answer, "I know, so tragic." But I would not embrace their pity. I might be numb with cold, but I would not ask for understanding. No, I would only sit muttering with envy for their broad umbrellas, their dryness, and the sweet, unwounded banality of their lives. But it would not matter. Couldn't, because the rain would still fall on the alleys and culverts where I'd rest. It would fall at the edges of parking decks where one might remain for a night or two before discovery. It would fall in the city parks where the leaves or bare branches would conspire with a cardboard sign to keep me dry, all legibility bled away from the pathetic messages I'd written on it. It would fall the way it fell in Al Tafar, soft and intermittently over the war, the rain's stops and starts becoming nothing more than weathered sighs of resignation.

When I imagined my death that night, sitting in a bunker at the eastern edge of the FOB, I imagined all of its possible permutations. I sipped from a bottle of Royal Horse and gazed out through the round entrance of the bunker, an aperture through which I could see the buildings and minarets tinged in purple and black by each variety of night passing through the hours. I imagined it all, the first wound coming soon, in fall or what would pass for winter, likely to be cold, apt to be. I'd bleed, to be sure, if I were not also concussed, boxed on the ears, and de- and re-pressurized in an instant. I would bleed. I'll bleed. I spoke out loud, slurring the words slightly, my voice echoing with a dull reverberation in the concrete tube. Murph would find my body, but first I had to become a body, so that there would be something to be shot, but more likely there would be an explosion, more likely there would be metal made into sheets with jagged edges folded over into my skin and my skin would be torn. And as confusion always seems to follow blasts, I would be left to bleed until my face became gray and my skin all over became gray and thus would I become a body. I said "gray" and "body" and my quiet vowels echoed out the ends of the short tube and I'd be dead and A and O sounds trickled into the night, into the slight rain, and I saw Murph. I was drunk. I saw Murph cradling my head, its new concavity, saw him drag me by my arms. My legs, limp and dead, dragged sputteringly along the ground, where they bounced at slight shifts in elevation, but I didn't notice them as they were dragged behind my body. I laughed and the soft expulsive H made no echo and I saw water and my body floating, my blood in it, and I thought I smelled my blood, my body, a ripe metallic. I was so drunk. I saw inside dark boxes, cheap tin caskets and Virginia and all the little graves lined up like teeth in the field and the dogwoods blooming and then the falling petals and my mother crying, she was crying. I made her cry. I saw the solidity of the earth, the worms, the flag and the tin box fading away and I saw brown earth forever and I thought of Murph and water and I mouthed the word "water" in a questioning tone and that is all I remembered before I woke up, all except the syllabic echo of my voice against the concrete going "qua, qua, qua."

The rain stopped. The weather mellowed. Our next forty-eight-hour rotation on patrol was uneventful. We were unaware of even our own savagery now: the beatings and the kicked dogs, the searches and the sheer brutality of our presence. Each action was a page in an exercise book performed by rote. I didn't care.

I hadn't talked to Murph in days. No one had. I found the remnants of his casualty feeder card and the letter and picture from his ex-girlfriend in a laundry bucket, soap and all. I put them in my pocket. I started tailing him, trying to figure out what he was up to. I didn't want to believe that I was watching the actions of someone who was already dead, so I searched for evidence that would contradict this; I searched for some grasp, at least, at life.

I began to find his mark all over the FOB: Murph was here. A little tag: two eyes and a nose peering over one thin line. Sometimes the fingers over the wall as well, sometimes not, but always the eyes and nose, ridiculous and searching, and the tag, Murph was here. I considered the possibility that he had been doing this all tour. There were never any dates, at least not on the half dozen or so I found, but I didn't believe that any of them were older than a week or so. I attempted to triangulate his where-abouts from those half-dozen tags, narrowing down the places he could be one by one. Over the next few weeks I tried a stakeout on the DFAC, a transportation com-pany, distant guard towers, even the hajji market that the brigade colonel had allowed to be set up on post so that we could further assist the native population by partici-pating in their local black market economies. I couldn't find him anywhere.

Out of ideas, I asked around. "Anybody know where Murph's been off to?"

"Naw, man," they'd say.

"How the fuck would I know?" said others.

I ran into Sterling, his feet resting on a short stack of sandbags, a porno mag shading his eyes from the dulled sun. "Hey, Sarge, you seen Murph around lately?"

"Yeah," he said. "He's been going up to the medics' station and eyeballing some bitch up there."

"At headquarters?" I asked.

"No, dummy," he replied. "He's eyeballing our medic, fat-ass Smitty."

"Oh, right. I'm going to head up there and see what he's up to."

"Your war today, Private," Sergeant Sterling said, and I

headed out of our area, ducking under the netting stretched from bunker to bunker and from connex to connex. I used my hands to keep the sagging fabric from falling over me like a shroud. Thin light rippled down through the voids and fell onto my hands and my body and fell onto the dusty track toward the little hill where the HQ medics' unit was quartered.

I chain-smoked my way up the base of the hill. A small clapboard chapel stood in the packed dust that stretched out over the majority of the base. The white painted boards were chipped and peeling from the abrasive wind, and a few trees rose out of their potting holes around its perimeter, not yet taken by the earth where they were planted for shade, then left to fend for themselves in the heat of summer. A helipad was roughly scoured out of the dirt at the top of the hill. Behind it a series of tents and exhumed concrete culverts sat in a sectioned maze. A low stone wall surrounded the entirety of the small compound, snaking along the crest of the hill like an unwound ribbon of decalcified bone, seeming on the verge of collapsing back into the earth from which the stones were taken.

The grade of the hill was gentle. I reached the top and looked back over the base and the fence line punctuated by towers and emplacements in the slight distance. Over the fence a road and a railway line ran together for a few hundred yards, edged by broad evergreens gone limp from the cool air and recent rain. Through those drooping branches the city sprawled out haphazardly like a drunk on a sidewalk, fallen where he may.

"Hey, Bart," Murph said.

He sat in the shade cast off by the wall, seemingly palsied against the unfinished outcroppings of stone.

"Where you been, buddy?" I asked.

"I've been here. Here."

"You OK?"

Murph's hands were in his pockets. His stretched-out legs crossed at the ankles. He seemed to be looking at the medics' station, waiting for some particular thing that I did not know about. The thwump, thwump of a chopper rolled out of the sky. The bird dipped and swayed in the air, coming in low over the horizon, out of the glare. I sat down next to him in the shadow of the wall, and we put our hands over our covers so they didn't blow off in the fine particles of dust swirling in little spirals over the compound beneath the rotor wash.

The compound began to bustle as soon as the chopper fixed its hover above the helipad. A medic guided the chopper in and two more medics had a stretcher at the ready. Even from our position at the wall we could see that it was stained rust brown with blood. Another medic, a girl, squatted in the dust next to the stretcher. She was blond and wore a brown T-shirt and latex gloves that reached up to her pale elbows. The short sleeves of her shirt were rolled up toward the gentle white arc of her shoulders, and her gloves were a shade of sky blue that stood out against the desert's dull wintry monochrome so vibrantly that we were transfixed by every minute motion that they made.

"You looking at this girl?" I asked.

"It's what I've been doing."

The chopper landed and the crew chief and the medics dragged a boy off the metal floor of the cabin, and he wailed in pantomime beneath the staccato beat of the spinning blades. His own blood followed his passage from the floor to their arms and onto the stretcher, and his left leg was no longer a leg but instead dangled like a coarse cornmeal mush the color of wet clay beneath his scissored pants. The girl's hands applied a tourniquet to the leg, and she took a position next to the stretcher and they ran beside it toward the makeshift hospital, and one gloved hand was in his hand and one gloved hand ran over his face, into his hair, over his lips and eyes, and they disappeared behind the tent cloth and the chopper took off, again listing in flight and receding off toward the horizon. As the whip of the rotors faded over the city, the boy's voice became louder as he screamed in the small enclosure of the hospital tent. The few people wandering near the hill stopped. Murph and I did not move or speak. All those gathered listened as the unavoidable sound of the boy's screams weakened and then died. We could only hope that his voice had broken, that it had become tired or had been anesthetized, that he now took deep breaths of cool air, his vocal cords unshaken by the music of his agony, but we knew it wasn't true.

"I want to go home, Bart," Murph said. He pulled out a dip, tucked it behind his lower lip and spit into the dust.

"Soon, man, soon," I said.

The passersby moved on, over and down the hill, reverted to their prior state.

"I'm never going to tell anyone I was here when we get home," he said.

"Can't help some people knowing, Murph."

The girl came out of the tent. All urgency subtracted from her movement. She peeled the gloves off, now splotched darkly with blood, and tossed them into a barrel. Her arms were pale, but her hands were dark, and I could see that they were small. I looked at Murph and I thought I knew why he had been coming here. It was not because she was beautiful, though she was. It was something else. We watched as she took a chunk of soap out of a dish and washed her hands in a makeshift sink bolted to a post. In the afternoon light, the soft down on her neck was visible and she was washed in the light. Sparse clouds floated by and she sat on the ground and lit a cigarette and she crossed her legs and began to cry quietly.

And I thought it was this and not her beauty that brought Murph there over those long indistinguishable days. That place, those little tents at the top of the hill, the small area where she was; it might have been the last habitat for gentleness and kindness that we'd ever know. So it made sense to watch her softly sobbing in the open space of a dusty piece of ground. And I understood why he came and why I couldn't go, not just then at least, because one never knows if what one sees will disappear forever. So sure, Murph wanted to see something kind, he wanted to look at a beautiful girl, he wanted to find a place where compassion still happened, but that wasn't really it. He wanted to choose. He wanted to want. He wanted to replace the dullness growing inside him with anything else. He wanted to decide what he would gather around his body, to refuse that which fell toward him by accident or chance and stayed in orbit like an accretion disk. He wanted to have one memory he'd made of his own volition to balance out the shattered remnants of everything he hadn't asked for.

The girl rose and tossed her cigarette on the ground, smothered it beneath the toe of her boot, and walked toward the chapel. She walked past the poplar and withered hackberry planted haphazardly about, toward the chapel, which rested like an afterthought in its dusty hollow, set back from the netting that covered the artillery pieces perched on the far side of the outpost's gentle summit. Light fell between the wood slats, passing from one side to the other through the gaps in the warped boards. Its steeple with its simple unadorned cross was visible even to the residents on the edge of the city. The girl in the distance was framed by the plain white structure, chipped and bruised.

There were no doors and the windows lacked both frame and glass. She tracked the fine dust as she walked and it rose up behind her in small plumes slightly as she went.

I put my hand on Murph's shoulder. "We're going to be cool," I said. "We've got each other. We know what's up."

"I don't want to be tight with anyone because of this. Being here can't be the reason we're tight. I won't let it be."

"Naw, man," I said. "You and me, we're tight just 'cause. We'd be tight anywhere. It isn't about this." I can't remember if I meant it. I felt so different then, with everything immediate and new, with no reflection, and I saw only with the short sight of looking for whatever might kill me in the next few moments. I don't even know if we were actually close. It was only after that I tried to understand, to discover what it was I was guilty of.

I clasped his hand in mine and pulled him up and we stood and walked back toward the platoon area. I knew what he was trying to say and it frightened me. He wouldn't be bound by this place to anything or anyone, even me. And I was afraid because I wondered what would be required for him to keep that promise to himself.

We did not take more than a few steps before we heard the whine of incoming mortars. A bright sound like the sky had become a boiling kettle. We looked at each other, Murph and I, dumbly staring into our own infinity made up of fractions upon fractions of seconds. For one brief incalculable moment we were not brave or afraid. Neither spoke nor moved. Welled eye abuts welled eye, a look between gun-broke horses. I couldn't tell where the first one hit, but it sounded close. It enveloped me, a small metal fist to the chest of the earth. The whole ground shook under my boots, and all I saw was a bright flash and then gray smoke flung like dirty paint on a washed-out canvas, all shapes beaded and dissipated by the angry crunch of the impact.

I hit the ground without thinking and covered my head with my hands, opened my mouth and crossed my ankles over each other. Count the heartbeats. Still there. Small pieces of metal flew over my head with each deep concussive impact, moving with a speed and sound that seemed beyond all governance. Take a breath. Then another. Getting harder now. Focus.

I gave up, surrendered, whatever, I was gone. My muscles became marionetted by nerve ending and memory. "Murph!" I heard the sound of my own voice, disembodied, arching into and out of the dust and smoke. "Murph!" No answer. The voice of my drill sergeant entered my mind, dominated each and every synapse as it fired inside my as yet unpunctured brain. Get small, Private. If your dumb ass wants to live, you get so fucking small you can take cover under your K-pot.

I didn't count the mortars. All measures of time and increment were discarded like childish superstitions. Crump. Crump. Crump. The earth shook and the vibrations ran up the heels of my palms where my hands, now bloodied, desperately tried to push the dry earth into a ridge in front of my face. They flowed up to my elbows and shook the buttons of my blouse, which dug like rivets into the ground. Get small, Private. You fucking get small and stay small.

There was a lull, brief and intangible like a small circle of sunlight falling absently through clouds. A deep constriction occurred in my chest, under my breastbone, as if my ribs had turned into fingers clutched in an arthritic fist. I was still prostrate on the ground. My face and body had plowed a small plot in which I lay. Dirt in my mouth ground against my teeth, coating my tongue with a thin particulate film. It was in my nose too. Each breath was thick and structural and I felt for a moment like I was falling, like falling into wakefulness after dreaming your fingers have slipped from their last nocturnal handhold.

I listened for an all clear but heard nothing. This is my life again, I thought. Fuck it, I'm not going to die in a grave dug by my own bleeding hands. I got up and as I rose to my knees the mortars began to fall again, though not so close as before. An adjustment of fire. No one was around to call out direction or distance, so I ran. I was afraid. My eyes welled with tears, and I wet my pants and though there was no need I shouted "I'm up" and took off on limbs of unset jelly. "I'm moving," I screamed, sobbing with each step, and, "I'm down," I said, out of breath and fallen into the womb of a low ditch running with dirty foul water that would not wash out for weeks. Only my nose and eyes were above the level of the water. A flock of babblers scattered in the distance, and the crumpling noise dissipated, fading with the mortars as they were walked away from my position. I heard the fragments tearing through the air again, hard and fast but not as close. I stayed in the shit water until I was sure that none had fallen for a little while. Gray smoke settled down into my fetid ditch. Fuck. I breathed. I made it.

I looked around and tried to figure out exactly where I'd ended up. The sewage ditch ran through the center of the base, below the hill where the chapel and the medics' station sat, just below another small rise where the colonel allowed the hajjis to set up little shops in a strip of abandoned buildings from before the war. The little shops that everyone on the FOB called the hajji mall must have been the mortars' intended target. It seemed they'd caught the brunt of the barrage. On the knoll above me, the hajjis arranged themselves supplicant, clutching at their wooden prayer beads. A chorus of grim wails began. Their little storefront hovels were on the brink of destruction, fires ablaze here and there, and parts of cheap knockoff watches had been scattered in the open spaces around the bazaar. Their bent and broken faces counted time without standard. Coils and springs, the bright silver and gold of counterfeit metal, were all sown errantly about, which made the freshly pocked earth glitter in the sun just so.

Like the dust, the smoke from the last of these mortars dissipated and floated away toward sparse clouds roughly brushstroked against the pale blue sky. A siren blared, warning of the already fallen mortars. I crawled out of the ditch and began to move toward the little burned bazaar, my boots sloshing with stale wetness.

In an open courtyard medics treated the wounded. A shopkeeper was lying in the dust, blood pulsing from his neck, black and jugular. His black eyes widened and then shut tightly. His feet kicked out wildly. Worn brown sandals conducted themselves through the dust, back and forth, leaving abstract markings on the ground like the hands of an obscene clock. The medics held his neck and applied pressure to the wound, unable to stop the bleeding until his body was spent of its supply and he wrenched one last time, the surface of his body now settling in the dust. He was surrounded by his fellow itinerant merchants, who shooed away the medics and lifted him onto their shoulders, his blood soaking their white shifts and the tails of their headdresses. One fetched a piece of plywood and laid it out on an inert fountain centered in the courtyard of their bazaar. They rested his body on the fountain and began an otherworldly recitation. The artillery pieces near the chapel began to buck and jump. Each pull of the lanyard sent shells screaming out toward the city. The ground was stained rust brown where the man died. The last tremors of his legs and arms left a strange impression in the earth. I got down on one knee for a closer look, but turned away, fighting convulsions of dry heaves and bile. The image burned into my mind like a landscape altered by erosive weather. Even as I walked away, I saw it, a perfect bloody angel made of dust.

I made my way uneasily toward the chapel. Its steeple had collapsed. The small wooden cross was broken and speared the earth near a clump of tamarisk trees. The girl was there, the medic, about where I expected her to be, lying on the ground next to the chapel, her hair blowing in small wisps behind her, in and out of the dust in a manner both fantastic and actual. Her eyes were half-lidded. The uniformed backs of two boys blanketed her in the performance of some ancient pantomime, a silent and shuffling attempt at recuperation.

One of them looked up at me when I reached them. "I think she's dead," he said. The other one turned around. It was Murph, sitting on his knees with his hands resting on his thighs, gape-jawed at the sight of her. "I just got here yesterday," the other one said. Murph was silent. He didn't move. "I didn't know what to do," the boy said, weeping now, and then shouting, "Where were the fucking medics?!" I reached over to him and grabbed him by the shoulders, standing him up.

"Come on, buddy," I said. "We've got to get her moved."

Two of the chapel's warped and battered planks had fallen on her and we reached over to pick them up. The force of the blast had torn her shirt open and a deep wound in her side had already ceased bleeding. Her skin was a pale gray.

Dead gray. We repositioned her shirt to cover her and laid out three planks parallel and placed her on them.

I tied off the planks with some rope and lifted her up. "Murph," I said. "Come on, give us a hand." The new private grabbed the back end near her feet while Murph curled up helplessly in the still-smoldering ruins of the chapel, muttering to himself, over and over again, "What just happened." As we walked her up the hill, his litany faded from our ears. The new boy and I walked the dead girl's body up to the medics' station.

We walked her past a copse of alder and willow that bowed in the heat of the small fires burning nearby, their old branches lamenting her, laid out as she was on that makeshift litter. Our hands began to cramp with each passing step, each taken with whatever reverence we could muster, clutching at the edges of the boards. Thin splinters roughed the flats of our palms as we walked. Listing in concert with our deliberate footsteps, the gentle curves of her body swayed beneath her torn clothes. The boards creaked. A small number of boys out on a head count stopped and turned toward us. A pale review as her body ascended the gently sloping hill, fringed by the bleached and spotted patterns of their uniforms. We conducted her pall in earnest up the remainder of the hill. At the top, we lowered her to the ground and set her under a tree on the tied-together boards, her body now translucent and blue-tinted. One of the soldiers alerted the medics and we watched them as they came to her. Her friends grabbed her and enveloped her in hugs and kisses. She rolled absently in their loving arms and they cried out beneath the setting sun. I held my hands to the back of my skull. As I walked away, the muezzin call began. The sun set like a clot of blood on the horizon. A small fire had spread from the crumbling chapel, igniting the copse of tamarisk trees. And all the little embers burned like lamps to light my way.

9

NOVEMBER 2005

Richmond, Virginia

BY THE TIME autumn came again I was firmly settled in the old gasworks building at the edge of the river. My life was small. I lived in an apartment on an upper floor and had little in the way of companionship. It was perfect for a while. A stray tortoiseshell cat would occasionally settle in an unkempt flowerbox hanging from my window. It had a habit of meandering over ledges and sills, jumping between air-conditioning units and the building's few balconies. I reached out once or twice and tried to pet it. "Here, buddy," I said, "here, kitty-kit," but it only mewed at me and continued rubbing its face on the stub of a naked branch. I'd strung a few medals above a small gas heating unit. The picture of Murph I'd taken from his helmet was tacked into a nook of broken plaster next to the window. I rarely went out.

Sometimes I'd cross the footbridge to the city side of the river to get a case of beer or a box of frozen potpies. On the way back I always noticed the diminished intervals between my footfalls, looking mostly down at the tops of my boots, how my gait had withered to a shuffle since I'd come home. When it got cold enough I'd rest a few beers on the windowsill overnight. I'd cook a potpie on a hot plate, as I was unequipped to follow the proper heating instructions. As night settled in, and frost spread on the edges of the windows, I'd flip through news stories in magazines picked out of garbage cans, searching for the names of places I had been. I'd eat a half-cooked meal and drink enough of the window-chilled beers to fall asleep. I often wondered what someone would see if they looked up from the river as it cut its habitual curve through the little valley, my arm above it, skinny and white, reaching through a yellowed curtain, a disembodied hand pulling in, from time to time, one last, yes just one last, beer before sleep.

In the mornings I'd walk up to the roof of the building and work the lever of a cheap rifle I'd picked up from Kmart, shooting at the refuse accumulating at the base of the building. Small trash fires sometimes began when a spark from the lead settled into ember on the cardboard and discarded fabrics below me. I traced the paths of birds in flight, following closely behind the creatures, embracing them in the two stakes of my sight post. But some reflexive tremor always overtook me and I'd work the action, over and over, expending the unfired cartridges to scatter on the tarred rooftop around my lawn chair.

That was more or less my life. I was like the curator of a small unvisited museum. I didn't require much of myself. I might return a small trinket from the war back to a shoebox, take another out. Here a shell casing, there a patch from the right shoulder of a uniform: articles that marked a life I was not convinced had needed to be lived.

I knew the C.I.D. investigators would find me eventually, and I was pretty sure I knew what they wanted. Someone had to be punished for what happened to Murph. It probably wouldn't matter what our level of culpability was. I was guilty of something, that much was certain, that much I could feel on a cellular level. What crimes we had committed, though, which articles we'd be charged under, didn't seem to matter. They'd find ones broad enough to fit over what it was we'd done, and justice would be served, and Murph's mother would be satisfied, would stop asking whether the army covered up the nature of her son's death.

And me? That letter? Five years was my guess. I only vaguely remembered the long cursory sessions of legal instruction in the auditorium during basic. The drill sergeants had seemed to really turn the screws on us the night before. Front-back-goes for hours in the barracks hallway, the morning run that turned our legs to quivering spindles, and when the JAG officer got up on stage to tell us everything that was expected of us according to the Uniform Code of Military Justice, all I can remember is being on the edge of sleep, feeling like I was floating in the cushioned theater chair and loving it. I'm not blameless. Some will say I should have known: goddammit, you were a soldier and you couldn't even stay awake? Well, see, I was no hero, no poster boy, I was lucky to get out upright and breathing. I'd been willing to trade anything for that. That's what my cowardice was: I accepted the fact that a debt would come due, but not now, please not now, anything for a little more time.

It happened so easily when the day came. Something turned. The note was called in. I remember the white sky and fog above the James, snow, unbelievably early for Virginia, beginning to fall over the hotels and abandoned tobacco warehouses, each flake a repetition of the one before as they descended through the veil of just how little I remembered, and my memory narrowing, the snow falling unmercifully as it spread over the river, the sky now white forever and unbroken and low.

Every moment has turned over in my mind since I came back from Al Tafar. Each one unlinked. But then it was just another day, the snow nothing more than a curious way to distinguish that day from the day before. I'd put my hands through the open window when it started and watched, untroubled, as each flake met my skin and melted, saw the river stones take on a thin sheet of blankness underneath the naked sycamore and dogwood trees that lined the avenue below. A car pulled up, a Mercury, I think, gray in color. A man stepped out. The small silver bars on his shoulders reflecting off an unknown light as he closed the door.

As I think about it now, all the times I think of the unceasing footfalls, the endless loop in which I watch him walking up the street, it seems as though I should have asked the snow to stop, for one reprieve, to not have to face another *next*. But even in my mind the fire of time still burns, just the same as it did then.

The knock came quickly after that. I opened my door, ashamed at the state of myself, unshaven, my life more or less ignored. There were times I'd been pleased with my ability to give up, to forget, to wait...for what? I don't know. The captain entered the room and stood looming over the emptiness in which I lived. I wore only a pair of PT shorts and an unwashed sleeveless undershirt, stained a little. It was cold. The snow filled the window with whiteness as though a shroud had been hung over it. A thin blanket hung from my shoulders and I stank. It had been weeks since I'd drawn a sober breath.

"John?" he asked softly.

"Yes, sir."

"I'm Captain Anderson, from C.I.D." He laid his hat down on the small table that more or less furnished the room. "Do you know why I'm here?"

"My mother said —"

"She said you left."

"I did."

He smiled. "You can't run from us, John. Anyway, we just want to talk."

Something about the way he spoke seemed strange. His voice was gentle, but it had a power and certainty behind it. I remembered that as he spoke, Mother Army also spoke. Tall and athletic-looking, he also carried the paunch of a tenured gym teacher who lives alone and washes down the sports news shows with a six-pack by himself. His eyes were a little worn down. He was old for captain's bars.

"You know LaDonna Murphy."

I didn't say anything.

He pulled a clear bag with an envelope inside it out of his inside jacket pocket. I could see that it had been torn open, roughly, hurriedly. "That wasn't a question," he said. He walked over to the wall where my few medals hung and looked at each one carefully, pausing for a few moments at the spot where I'd tacked up the photo of Murph.

"You wrote this letter."

I didn't know what to say. If writing it was wrong, then I was wrong. If writing it was not wrong, enough of what I'd done had been wrong and I would accept whatever punishment it carried. I was ready. Everything I could recall about the war flashed kaleidoscopically, and I closed my eyes and I felt the weight of time wash over my body. I could not pattern it. None of it made sense. Nothing followed from anything else and I was required to answer for a story that did not exist.

The call of a whip-poor-will outside the window opened my eyes. The captain had not moved. And I could not comprehend what separated one moment from the next, how each breath I took would somehow be made into a memory, assigned its own significance, and set aside as the vast material I was left to make an answer from.

He waited, then said, "What, you've given up?"

"No."

"Not what it looks like."

"It's different out there now."

"No it's not. You're different."

"No one cares."

"So what?"

"I don't know how to live out there anymore."

"Hmmm...I was well acquainted with that idea back when it was just called cowardice. Have you seen the doctors?"

"Yeah, I saw them."

I remembered the long, weatherless February in Kuwait waiting for an unknown period of sequestration to be over, to go home, home. Day after day of staring into the desert stretched out on all sides like an ocean of twice-burned ash. We would be evaluated. Our ability to reenter the world would be assessed. The company was herded into a huge canvas tent. Clipboards and pencils and sheets of paper handed down the rows of boys on benches, dress right, dress. Outside the desert still expanded, slowly chewing foliage up the way a wave breaks on a shore, toward disinterested and inescapable infinity, but we were glad to be so far south of Al Tafar: hors de combat. The benches on which we sat were planted firmly in the sand and off toward the distant end of the tent an officer began to speak.

"Boys, you have fought properly and were well led, so you are alive. Now you are being sent home."

I had in me a profound disquiet.

"I will ask you to fill out the form affixed to the clipboard in front of you. This form will measure your level of stress." He paused and pulled on the bottom of his starched blouse, straightening out the untidy folds. "Any man who feels that he is suffering from any kind of, oh, disorder, can be assured that he will receive the best mental hygiene care that the government can afford. More conveniently..."

I began looking at the questions as he spoke, forgetting my place and immersing myself in the ramifications of the questions and the possible mental deterioration that might be in store for me. I ignored the dust, the haughty speech of the officer and the odd warmth of the February air.

Question one: Were you involved in combat actions?

I checked yes.

Question two: After a murder-death-kill, rate your emotional state and indicate it by checking one of the following boxes:

A. Delighted

B. Malaise

The officer was still speaking. "We have this questionnaire down to an exact science. If it is determined that you are overly stressed, you will be given the opportunity to re-cuperate in the presence of the best doctors available. You won't even have to leave. You will go home when you are cured and have recovered your requisite hard-on for your country." He laughed a little after the last part, as if to let us know he was still our brother, that Mother Army still loved us just as much as she always had, and wasn't it funny that we had to jump through these hoops in the first place.

I thought of something Sergeant Sterling had said after Murph died. Fuck 'em. Yes. Fuck 'em, my new design for liv-ing. I checked A. I went home.

"Yeah, I wrote it," I said, finally answering the captain's ques-tion.

"Sir," he said, his tone changing ever so slightly.

"Y'all don't have me anymore."

"We can have you anytime we want, Private." He took the letter out of the envelope. The slight sound of the paper unfolding filled the room as he began to read: "Mom, every-thing is going well here, Sgt. Sterling is taking care of us…"

"Stop it."

"What?"

"Stop. I said I wrote it."

"You know it was wrong?"

"I guess."

He shook the letter. "We know what happened now. We know what you did."

"I didn't do anything."

"Not what we heard. Why don't you give us your side of it?"

"Doesn't matter."

The captain laughed and began to pace around the room.

I felt like scum then, worse, and still do, so sometimes, on days when I remember well, when there is a deer gone down to drink in the creek behind my cabin, and I get my rifle out and for the hundredth time don't shoot the thing and just sit there starting to tremble and then the sun is out, I'll realize I can't smell any of it, not the burned powder, not the metal on fire, not the rank exhaust or the lamb or the stink of shit in the Tigris, where we waded up to our thighs that day. I think maybe it was my fault, fuck, I did it, no it didn't happen, well, not like that, but it's hard to say sometimes: half of memory is imagination anyway.

The captain wouldn't tell me everything, only that there had been an incident. Civilians had been killed, and so on. Sterling had gone on leave just before it had gotten the attention of some higher-ups who felt they needed to come down hard on someone to prove that all these boys with guns out roaming the plains of almost every country in the world would be accountable. And Sterling never made it back to be accountable.

So it was a rumor that had brought the captain to see me, the underlying truth of the story long since skewed by the variety of a few boys' memories, perhaps one or two of them answering with what they wanted the truth to be, others likely looking to satisfy the imagined needs of a mother, abused and pitied as a result of that day in Al Tafar, which sometimes seems so long ago.

Thinking about him now, I've come to realize that Sergeant Sterling was not one those people for whom the existence of others was an incomprehensible abstraction. He was not a sociopath, not a man who cared only for himself, seeing the lives of others as shadows on a thinly lit window. My guess was that he'd been asked a question and he had answered it as broadly as he could, not thinking of all the room he'd left for the gaps to be filled in by the men who had asked it.

But I still believe in Sterling now because my heart beats. A lie by anyone on his behalf is an assertion of a desire to live. What do I care about the truth now? And Sterling? The truth is he cared nothing for himself. I'm not even sure he would have realized he was permitted to have his own desires and preferences. That it would have been OK for him to have a favorite place, to walk with satisfaction down the long, straight boulevards of whatever post he may have gone to next, to admire the uniformity of the grass, green and neatly shorn beneath a blue, limitless sky, to bury himself in a sandy shoal in the shallow of some clear cold stream and let the water wash over the pitted skin of his scarred body. I don't know what his favorite place would have been like, because I don't believe he would have let himself have one. He would have waited for one to be assigned to him. That's the way he was. His life had been entirely contingent, like a body in orbit, only seen on account of the way it wobbles around its star. Everything he'd done had been a response to a preexisting expectation. He'd been able to do only one thing for himself, truly for himself, and it had been the last act of his short, disordered life.

As soon as the captain closed his teeth around the hard "t" ending "accident," I closed my eyes. When I closed them I saw Sergeant Sterling on the side of a mountain. Saw the rifle barrel in his mouth. Saw the way he went limp, so limp in that impossible moment when the small bullet emerged from his head. Saw his body slide a few feet down the mountain, the worn soles of his boots coming to rest in a clot of pine needles. Then I opened them.

"So that's it, huh?" I asked.

He came over to me and put his hand on my shoulder. I could see he was fingering a pair of handcuffs underneath his overcoat. "You're gonna be OK, John," he said. "Trust me."

"There are lies all through this."

"It's just the way it's gotta be, kid. Someone has to answer for some of it."

"Shit rolls downhill, huh, Captain?"

"Shit's rolling everywhere nowadays. It's a shitty goddamn war. You ready?"

I put my hands out, wrists up, and he clicked the cuffs in place in front of me. "You'll be all right," he said again.

"I just wish more of it was true," I said.

"Me, too, but it's lies like this that make the world go 'round."

"You mind if I take something with me?"

"Go ahead, but they'll take it from you when we get there."

"That's all right," I said. I walked over and picked up Murph's casualty feeder card and my own and tucked them into the elastic band of my PT shorts.

He led me down through the cool dampness of the stairwell and out into the street. His car was parked on the road across the footbridge and I asked if we could stop a minute when we got to the middle of the bridge. I threw the two cards into the river awkwardly and watched them until they had floated past the old railroad trestles downstream and disappeared far out of sight. It was still early. The sun had not yet broken up the mist over the river, and the sky was still white as if heavy with snow. I turned toward the line of trees across the river and saw the whole world in fractions of seconds like the imperceptible flicker of light between frames of film, the long unrecorded moments that made up my life, one after another, like a movie I never realized had been playing all along.

10

OCTOBER 2004

Al Tafar, Nineveh Province, Iraq

MURPH, GAPE-JAWED AND crying, was gone. He left after finding the medic's body sprawled in a spot of sunlight that fell through a hole the mortar made in the broken chapel's roof. The tall grass was speckled with her blood. He wasn't at her ceremony, where the brigade sergeant major stood her rifle between her boots and rested her small unblemished helmet at the top. He'd already left through a hole in the wire by then, his clothes and disassembled weapon scattered in the dust.

He was gone but we didn't know it yet. We lazed around our platoon area half-asleep beneath the light of a moon that cast shadows over the plywood guard tower and triple-strand concertina. Nothing told us this night would be different from any other until a few hours later when Sergeant Sterling calmly walked into the middle of our imperfect circle and said, "Someone had a big old bowl of dumbass today. Get your shit together." He'd looked annoyed by our random arrangement. Some of us were lying down, some were upright; some grouped together, some sat a little off, alone. It was hard to tell what bothered him more: his boys sprawled out like we'd been spilled carelessly from a child's toy box, a shitty head count, or the fact that one of us was missing. The incoming alarm sounded over the FOB, warning us of an event that had already happened, as usual. "Let's go get him," he said.

We assembled quickly, gathered our rifles and prepared to advance into the city of Al Tafar. At every gate soldiers poured out into the alleys and neighborhoods, the last echoes of a hundred chambering rifles ringing through the evening heat. As we made our way out into the first fringes of the city, windows showing lit rooms were blacked with a shuffle of curtains. Our barrels moved from place to place. Dogs wilted into shadow as we passed. The city, past curfew, seemed vast and catacombed, its black alleys a tightly wound maze. It was impossible to know whether we'd be back in an hour or a week; if we'd come back as one body or if we'd leave remnants of ourselves out along the dank canals or in the dry fields. Nothing was certain. Plans seemed ridiculous, as did effort. We were tired, and it seemed that we finally knew how tired we were. We trickled out into the city like water wrung from a mop until we'd gone about a thousand meters toward the bridge over Highway 1. Eventually, a man emerged with hands raised high from a doorway. A spare jangling sounded as twenty rifles paused on him at once.

"Mister, mister, don't shoot, mister," he pleaded. His language came glottal and broken. His fear was obvious as he stood there shaking, his body framed by the soft light in the doorway. "I see the boy," he said.

We bound him and sat him on the ground against the block wall of his home and called for a translator, who arrived masked in a black hood with holes cut out for his eyes and mouth. They began to chatter back and forth. Our eyes circled the street, bounced from window to streetlight, from the bent roadside trees to the darkest patches of the night. The translator had his knees on the man's thighs and his hands gripped his dirty shift, his body language telling us the nature of the questioning: Where is he? What do you know?

He stopped near his home to buy some apricot halawa for his wife. He and his friend the shopkeeper were talking of the heat and family and the occupation. He had his back to the street when the shopkeeper went stiff and pale, eyes wide and glossy. He put his money on the table and turned around very slowly.

From the train tracks that edged the outpost, a foreign boy walked naked, his shape lacking all color except for where his hands and face were tanned to a deep brown by the sun. He walked as a ghost, his feet and legs bleeding from his walk through the wire and detritus.

The man looked at us as he recounted this. His face pleaded, as though we could unlock some riddle for him. As he spoke, his bound hands waved. He paused for breath, finally, and put his hands on his head and said in his broken English, "Mister, why the boy walk naked?" as if we knew and were keeping it from him out of cruelty.

Someone nudged the translator. He barked at the man to continue. He said that Murph walked toward them directly. Where he crossed the street, he left bloody footprints in the pale dust. When he reached them, he raised his head absently to the sky and paused.

We imagined the soft blue of his eyes rimmed red with tears and the city appearing bent in the warmth of the evening and the dry breeze blowing the smells of sewage and cured lamb and the cool moisture of the river nearby.

Murph shuffled his feet at them, and swayed gently from side to side, his body flecked in sweat. He showed no awareness of their presence. It was as if the basic forms of the city, the angles and composition of its softly colored evening hues, were there for him to take in: a quiet stroll through an enormous museum gallery.

Sergeant Sterling gave voice to our impatience. "Where the fuck is he?"

"Ooohh," the man responded furtively, "I don't know." They had attempted to break Murph's trance, screamed and pleaded with him to return to the outpost. But as they screamed, the boy's eyes caught the shape of an old beggar. He turned and looked through them both for what seemed to be an endless moment, then walked off.

The eyes of the two men followed Murph as he walked clothed in nothing but the soft wattage of the streetlights, his form seemingly blinking as he passed from darkness into wan and flickering circles of light, then back into darkness. The huddled beggar scoured the garbage heaps on the fringes of a traffic circle. Murph walked through the roundabout and cars screeched to a halt as he passed balefully in front of their headlights. Before he reached the other side, all of the cars in the circle had stopped. Men opened doors and stood on the edges of their floorboards and watched him in stunned silence, the only noise the shoddy cylinders of their engines turning.

When they last saw him, the bleeding boy approached the beggar, who in his sackcloth still crouched down warily, gathering his pastiche of discarded melon rinds and bread crusts. A knot of flies swarmed about his head, glittering in the yellow light cast off the streetlights of their audience, and the beggar took no pause to shoo them. The man said that he and the shopkeeper were like all the others, stunned and amazed by what they'd seen. Spotlit against the wall of an old crumbling hovel, the old man grabbed Murph by the hand and led him into the dark.

He looked to the interpreter and then to us. "They go down the alley…gone." We cut him free of his bindings, then turned northwest toward the circle. Our boots impacted softly against the dust, which settled like lime on the legs of our pants. Birds and shadows were caught quickly by our eyes, then returned to a fluttering periphery of hollow noises: a motor in the distance, an old man breathing from a doorway, the tails of his wife's robes softly dragging across a mud floor. We moved until over the crest of a low rise we saw lights splayed out in all directions.

We neared the circle and spread out on its edge. A daze had set in on the roundabout's occupants. They walked back and forth between one another's cars, speaking in low voices, hands pointing wildly as if to map out the strange turns that life, in peculiar moments such as this, can take.

Before entering into the light of the circle, we checked our weapons and determined likely threats. Someone shrugged. We rose out of the fringes of the dark, our forms modular and alien to the men standing there. Most of them ran off. We knew they ran for fear of us, so we didn't follow them. Others got in their cars and peeled loudly down the street, their antique engines high and whistling, the smell of rubber adding to the odor of decomposition that permeated the air.

We searched the perimeter of the circle. The streetlights gave off a shallow hum. The abandoned cars were warm and made little ticking noises at irregular intervals. We looked for signs of Murph in the shadows, some indication of his passage. In a hidden alley, obscured by a tattered green awning, a private called out.

On his knees, he sifted through a pile of discarded fruit, rotten and blanketed by a collection of flies. We walked over to him and watched as he kneaded his hands through the soggy mass. Flies battered him lightly. He made a small clearing in the alley and a puddle showed itself blackly against the spoiled citrus. The smell of copper stagnated and mixed with the remnants of the beggar's scavenged fruit.

"That's blood," someone said. A light shined down the alley. We followed the footprints, which gently reflected the light, directing us toward a maze that vanished down staircases and around unmapped corners. We checked our weapons again, quietly reasserting our confidence under the whispering noise of metallic levers shifting position, and walked down the alley.

In the dark, a swallow illustrated the turns with its call's echo. It guided us to a hub, where the alley branched off in several directions. An old man gauzed in dusty sackcloth and smelling of rotten fruit lay prostrate in the center. Someone tapped at him with his boot. No response. The blood, not yet congealing, adhered to the boy's boot and dripped in the moonlight. We turned the beggar over. The stench of calloused and picked-at sores, now burst from the beating he had taken, overpowered us. The gray of pallor mortis settled quickly over his wrinkled skin, becoming paler and paler as we stood there.

Sergeant Sterling chewed his bottom lip in the dark over the indrawn form of the dead man, his hands stuck casually in his pockets. His rifle hung loosely from its sling.

"What now?" we asked.

Sterling looked back and shrugged. "Shit, I ain't got a clue."

The dead man seemed to move for a moment as we stood there, but it was only an effect of the rigor, the slight contraction of dead muscles over his brittle bones. It seemed impossible to know which path to take. We scoured the stonework for signs of footprints. The fear began to set in that Murph had bled out on his journey and been swept up into the arms of captors, too weak to resist, as helpless as a child asleep in the wilderness. We could not avoid thinking of him sleeping in that alley, being found by men who would take him to a basement, burn him and beat him, cut off his balls and cut his throat, make him beg for death.

We followed one soldier as he walked west toward the sloping banks of the river. It was as good a guess as any other. A mosque's towering minarets fooled the eyes and appeared to curve and hover over everything.

The sun began to rise. Colors, dull and bathed in the pale light, spread over the city in a palette of gray and gold and washed-out pastels. The morning heat began to swell our brains as we neared the river. We knew other units were searching for Murph. We heard the rattle of gunfire and the occasional reverberant slam of IEDs. But we encountered no resistance. The people we saw parted before us as quickly as they could. We walked down either side of a broad avenue that was lined by the hulks of cars set on fire in some recent past.

On the outskirts of the city we approached an open square. Two black mutts of indeterminate parentage heeled at the feet of their master. His dogs and his white shift stood out in the fallow bleakness. He affixed a three-legged mule to a cart. A wood-hewn contraption stood substitute for the mule's stumped right foreleg. He glanced at us, twenty heavily armed soldiers, and looked back disinterestedly to his work on the cart. We sent our interpreter to see what information, if any, he could give us. Then we waited, seated lazily about the square aiming our rifles at the few open windows and down the empty side streets.

They exchanged words, and the cartwright turned toward one of the side streets and pointed out a minaret of the mosque we had passed earlier. It jutted precariously over the bank of the river, a protuberance of mottled stone. There was nothing between us and the tower but a road and barren fields.

Sergeant Sterling fiddled with his sight aperture, flipping it back and forth from night sight to day sight while trying to decide what we should do. Finally, he spit onto the dusty road and said, "They ain't much for crop rotatin', are they?" He paused again. "What's he saying?" he asked the interpreter.

"He saw some men he didn't know going into the minaret last night."

"How many?"

"Five. Maybe six."

"They look strange or anything?"

The interpreter looked confused. "Compared to what?"

Sterling squatted down on the backs of his calves. "All right, you guys set up a perimeter here," he said to the rest of the platoon. "Me and Bartle are gonna check it out. It's probably nothing."

The cartwright offered to guide us to the tower. He led, followed by his elaborately improvised mule drawing the whole of his earthly possessions. He goaded the mule along. It consented with patient eyes and marked his path with a tripartite staccato of hoofbeats, the blunted wood of his other leg capped with wrappings of molded leather. In the back of his cart, a worn prayer mat covered a few pots of clay and stone. Items of cast iron wobbled about, shaking among a collection of woven figurines beaded in natural shades of turquoise and crimson and green.

On the side of the road a tree rose out of the otherwise sterile field, bent and swaying softly in the stale breeze. The smell of the river got stronger as we approached the minaret, a sweet coolness we had long forgotten. Past the tree and the smell of the river, the faded pink and blotchy minaret loomed at an odd angle, a dominant line through the corners of my eyes. The hermit tapped at the mule's hindquarter with a long crook of charred cedar, communicating in this fashion a command for the mule to halt. The mule brought his momentum to a stop and as the cart rolled its last few feet, the mule hopped on its wooden contrivance, its face a picture of stillness and calm.

The hermit took off his sandals and placed them in the

back of the cart. He slowly wiggled his toes, as if to stretch them for his journey. Looking from side to side several times, perhaps to assure himself of his place in the world, he walked to the front of the cart, where his hobbled mule breathed quietly. He gave it a pear, slowly stroking its muzzle as the mule chewed and addressed the man with its black eyes. He walked out into the dusty field toward the lone tree and, finding a large and appropriately angled root, reclined in the shade of its overhanging branches.

I looked at Sterling and shrugged. He shrugged back and called to the hermit from the side of the road, his voice echoing heavily over the short distance in the heat of late morning. Our shoulders hung limp against our sides.

The hermit called back, and as he did, the interpreter related what he said with a precise delay, which added to the confusion, their voices echoing in a way that gave me momentary déjà vu.

"He says that he has come through this place already and does not wish to walk the same way again." The voice of the man slightly distant fell off before the last words of Pidgin English came. We looked quizzically at the interpreter and he said, "Check over there," pointing to a patch of vegetation beneath the minaret.

Sterling motioned to the interpreter. "All right, get the fuck out of here. Head back to the others."

"I don't know, Sarge. Something ain't right. This seems off," I said. "Feels like a setup."

He looked at me with extraordinary calm. "C'mon, Private, I figured you'd know by now. 'Ain't right' is exactly what we're looking for."

I waited.

"Ah, fuck it," he said. "Only one way to find out."

We had looked for him hard, this one boy, this one name and number on a list. As the man pointed, our fears had become facts, our hopes smothered and mute. We had, in a strange way, surrendered. But to what, we did not know. The sound of gunfire could still be heard periodically in the distance. The city would be covered with brass casings. Battered buildings would have new holes. Blood would be swept into the streets and washed into gutters before we were through.

We looked at the old man in the field reclining peacefully beneath the shade of the tree and saw for the first time the depth of his age and his black eyes and the mysteries housed in them. His white shift fluttered and he laughed and swatted away a few bees with his hand. We turned and walked toward the copse of trees and bushes that ringed the tower.

At the base of the tower the trees and flowers were thin and tinder-dry. The tower itself rose upward and was slung out precariously over the river. Sterling and I circled the base of the tower in the heat of the nooning sun, its mass appearing out of the dirt and dead flora like some kind of ancient exclamation. We found Murph, finally, covered in a patch of lifeless hyacinth, resting motionless in the shade of the grass and low branches.

Laid up hard and broken-boned in the patch of vegetation that was his journey's end, his body was twisted at absurd angles beneath the pink and shimmering tower. We moved the brush that either wind or passersby had scattered over him. We uncovered his feet first. They were small and bloody. A supply sergeant could have looked at them and said size seven, but he would not need boots now. Looking to the top of the tower, it was clear that he fell from a window where two speakers had been set up to amplify the muezzin's call.

Daniel Murphy was dead.

"Not so high up, if you really think about it," Sterling said.

"What?"

"I think he was probably dead before he fell. It just isn't that great a height."

It was truly not a fall from all that great a height: broken bones were broken further, no resistance or attempt to land was made; the body had fallen, the boy already dead, the fall itself meaning nothing.

We pulled Murph free from the tangle of brush and laid him out in some shadow of respectability. We stood and looked him over. He was broken and bruised and cut and still pale except for his face and hands, and now his eyes had been gouged out, the two hollow sockets looking like red angry passages to his mind. His throat had been cut nearly through, his head hung limply and lolled from side to side, attached only by the barely intact vertebrae. We dragged him like a shot deer out of a wood line, trying but failing to keep his naked body from banging against the hard ground and bouncing in a way that would be forever burned into our memories. His ears were cut off. His nose cut off, too. He had been imprecisely castrated.

He'd been with us for ten months. He was eighteen years old. Now he was anonymous. The picture of him that would appear in the newspaper would be of him in Class A's in basic, a few pimples on his chin. We'd never be able to see him that way again.

I took my woobie out of my pack and covered him. I couldn't look anymore. Most of us had seen death in many forms: the slick mess after a suicide bomber, headless bodies gathered in a ditch like a collection of broken dolls on a child's shelf, even our own boys sometimes, bleeding and crying as it became apparent that the sound of a casevac was thirty seconds too far in the distance. But none of us had seen this.

"What should we do with him?" I asked. The words themselves seemed incomprehensible. I drifted in and around the significance of the question, first reckoning with the fact that the decision would be ours. Two boys, one twenty-four, the other twenty-one, would decide what should happen to the body of a boy who had died and been butchered in the service of his country in an unknown corner of the world.

We knew that if we brought him back, there would be questions. Who found him? What did he look like? What was it like?

"Fuck, little man. You didn't have to go out like this," Sterling said to the body at his feet. He flopped down on his butt into the dry grass and took his helmet off.

I sat next to Murph and began to tremble, rocking back and forth.

"You know what we got to do."

"Not like this, Sarge."

"It's what we do. No matter what. You know that shit, Bart."

"It'll be worse."

"We don't decide. That's way above our pay grade."

"Sarge, you gotta trust me. We can't let that happen."

We both knew what that was. There are few real mysteries in life. The body would be flown to Kuwait, where it would be mended and embalmed as best it could by mortuary affairs. It would land in Germany, tucked into a stack of plain metal caskets as the plane refueled. It would land in Dover, and someone would receive it, with a flag, and the thanks of a grateful nation, and in a moment of weakness his mother would turn up the lid of the casket and see her son, Daniel Murphy, see what had been done to him, and he would be buried and forgotten by all but her, as she sat alone in her rocking chair in the Appalachians long into every evening, forgetting herself, no longer bathing, no longer sleeping, the ashes of the cigarettes she smoked becoming long and seeming always about to fall to her feet. And we'd remember too, because we would have had the chance to change it.

He stood up and started pacing. "Let's just think this through a minute," he said. "Let me get a smoke."

I gave him one and lit one for myself. My hands were shaking and my lighter wouldn't stay lit in the wind and the wind blew the woobie and uncovered what was left of Murph's face. Sterling stared at the empty sockets. I put the blanket back. Minutes ticked into the past. A few birds darted in and out of the brush and sang. The sound of the river became clearer.

"You better not be wrong about this."

I couldn't think. I wanted to take it all back. "This is so fucked, Sarge."

"Chill out, man. Just chill out, all right," he said, and then paused reflectively. "Here's what we do: you get on that radio and tell the terp to send over the hajji with the cart. Tell them we didn't find him."

I took a minute and collected myself. Sterling went on, "We're gonna have to fix this like it never happened. You know what that means, right?"

"Yeah. I know."

"You sure?"

"I'm sure."

We waited. A strange peace took shape between us. The

sun muted the periphery into a mere abstraction of color and shape. Everything we did not look at directly became a blur in the corners of our eyes. We watched the hermit come, tapping lightly at the haunch of his mule. He walked slowly in the heat and all that was clear in our vision was the man and his lame mule emerging out of a hazy mirage, everything else vague or inverted or duplicate. The mule treaded lightly on its tinkered foreleg, and the man patiently guided it toward us. As he came closer we saw that the two mutts from before loped along behind him. The hermit approached and looked each of us in the eye as if we were lined up for an open-rank inspection, and finally said, "Give me a cigarette, mister." I gave him one and he lit it, inhaled deeply and smiled.

Sterling reached for Murph's legs and tried to lift him up. We didn't have the chance to take it back. We had never had the chance, not really. It was as if we had already done it in another life I could only vaguely remember. The decision had been made. I moved to where Sterling was and grabbed Murph by the arms. I shuddered quickly. My heart beat recklessly. We picked Murph up and brushed the dancing flies from his skin and tried not to look into his empty sockets as we laid him in the back of the cart among the clay and stone and the figurines of straw.

"We'll take him to the river," Sterling said. "We'll leave him there. Give me your lighter, Bart."

I did. He lit the Zippo and left it burning and dropped it into the dry brush at the base of the tower.

"Let's go," he said.

It was not far from the river, and we walked behind the hermit as he led the mule into some approximation of a trot. We followed behind this odd coterie of man and mule and dog for a half a klick or so, until we saw the banks of the river. Water lapped the edges and bulrushes swayed gently in the shallows at the banks.

Sterling tapped on my shoulder, pointed behind me, and I saw the minaret in flames from the dried brush burning at its base. Burn it. Burn the motherfucker down. The tower lit up like a flickering candle as the sun began to descend from its brutal apex. I thought for a moment that we might burn down the whole city for that one tower. I was briefly ashamed, but quickly forgot why.

Sterling looked at me and whispered, mostly to himself, "Fuck 'em, man. Fuck everyone on earth."

Amen. We floated behind the cart down the broad avenue leading to the edge of the river. The street was lined with poplars and the bodies from our search; opaque shades of brown, all ages and species. We walked past many things in flames. The thin and knotty trees and flowers soaked up the fire and lined the avenue in the descending sun like ancient guideposts, all flaming and circling a little light on the scattered bodies, breaking up the dark.

We floated past the people of the city, the old and childless hovel dwellers who wailed some Eastern dirges in their warbling language, all of them sounding like punishments sung specifically for our ears. Daniel Murphy's body in the cart reflected the orange glow, the only color on his thin and parchment skin was the flickering palette of the fire. The shadows danced on his pale form and only the listing of the broken mule and tottering cart made his body appear to move like something other than a canvas for this burning scene.

We walked the body in the cart down to the edge of the river. The hermit walked around to the rear of his cart, stroked the mule's flank and then embraced Murph, lifting him out of the flat carriage. Sterling and I each grabbed a leg and we walked the last few steps to the river and laid him in. He floated off quickly in the steady current, and in the water past the bulrushes little pools formed where his eyes had been.

"Like it never happened, Bartle. That's the only way," Sterling said.

"Yeah, I know." I looked at the ground. The dust blowing in fine swirls around my boots. I knew what was coming.

Sterling shot the cartwright once, in the face, and he crumpled to the ground. No time to even be surprised by it. The mule began to pull the cart, unbidden, as if by habit. The two dogs followed it into the coming night. We looked back toward the river. Murph was gone.

11

APRIL 2009

Fort Knox, Kentucky

THEN IT WAS spring again in all the spoiled cities of America. The dark thaw of winter fumbled toward its end and passed. I smelled it reeking through my window during that seventh April of the war, the third and last of my confinement. My life had become as ordinary as I could have hoped for. I was happy. The prison was only tier II, for convicts serving terms of five years or less, a Regional Confinement Facility, which all the Joes called "adult day care." It made me laugh.

I had been pleasantly forgotten about by almost everyone. The staff allowed me to check out books from the moderately well run prison library. I learned that when I finished reading them they could be stacked on the metal desk that jutted out of the cell wall and I'd be able to look out the window, which was large enough to let in light but far too high to see out of without the aid of something else to stand on. I had a fine view of the exercise yard and the tree line past the concertina fence, which more or less marked the limit of the base's prison grounds, for as long as I could balance on the ever-weakening bindings of whatever stacks of books allowed my looking. Beyond the tree line the dull world that ignored our little pest of a war rolled on.

My first few months inside, I spent a lot of time trying to piece the war into a pattern. I developed the habit of making a mark on my cell wall when I remembered a particular event, thinking that at some later date I could refer to it and assemble all the marks into a story that made sense. I still remembered what some of them meant for a long time afterward: that long chalky scratch below the mirror next to "FTA" stood for that kid whose head Murph cradled in the orchard as he died. The one above my bunk reflected an instant of thought I'd had in an alley in Al Tafar, in the heat of that first summer when the shade of webs of power lines were little blessings as we passed beneath them, and a corner was turned by whoever had been on point that day, and I saw Sterling as he turned around and waved for me and Murph to cross into the open road, and it occurred to me that Murph had had a choice, there were two paths he could have taken and I was one of them, and I asked myself if I could be worthy of that task, and wondered if that is what his mother meant when she asked me to take care of him, and is that why she asked? As I made my mark, if I remember right, the chalk broke and the mark became much shorter than I could recall intending, and what did it mean that this choice was an illusion, that all choices are illusions, or that if they are not illusions, their strength is illusory, for one choice must contend with the choices of all the other men and women deciding anything in that moment? I'd made that mark into a kind of flash, an explosion in chalk dust on the light green painted concrete of my walls. Who could ask to have their will be done against all that? And what about the choices we don't ever get to, like Murph's, which was not and will not be gotten to because he died, like me being that which was not gotten to? It seemed silly, but I remembered that mark and what it meant. Eventually, I realized that the marks could not be assembled into any kind of pattern. They were fixed in place. Connecting them would be wrong. They fell where they had fallen. Marks representing the randomness of the war were made at whatever moment I remembered them: disorder predominated. Entropy increased in the six-by-eight-foot universe of my single cell. I eventually accepted the fact that the only equality that lasts is the fact that everything falls away from everything else.

Sometimes the staff would come by my cell and see a new collection of marks. They were never able to distinguish new marks from old ones, but a few of the guards had a sense of what the volume was before they'd gotten their forty-eight hours off, or gone on vacation, and they recognized, if nothing else, when the randomness expanded. Now, I understand why they would have seen this as a pattern, and perhaps there was a pattern there after all, for I confess myself that had I been confined for another year or two the walls would have been full, there would have been no marks at all, just a wash, a new patina whitening the walls with marks of memories, all running together as if the memories themselves aspired to be the walls in which I was imprisoned, and that seemed just to me, that would have been a worthy pattern to have made. But it was not to be. Everything disrupts. The guards seemed to understand that my marks had meaning, so surely they can be forgiven if their error was one of interpretation.

They'd ask, "Getting near to your earliest possible release date, right?"

"Sure," I'd say. "Seems like I must be."

"Ah. You're a shoo-in for early release, a model prisoner."

"We'll see, I guess, but thanks."

"How many days you got down?" they'd ask, pointing to the marks on the walls, what I then would realize could appear to be an accounting of the passing days.

"Must be nine eighty-three, nine ninety, right? Almost a thousand?" they'd say and smile.

"Must be," I'd say, thinking of Murph, who was not counted for a while, wondering what his number would have been if I hadn't lied about it all.

His mother came to see me once, that spring before I was released. I could see that she'd been crying as she waited for me to come into the visiting area.

"Y'all can't touch, but I can get you coffee if you want," the guard said.

I didn't know what to say to her at first, but it seemed unfair that she had to bear it like this, to be responsible to start, so far away from any comfort or understanding. And if she should accuse, then I should be accused. His absence from the family plot was my fault. I had left him in the river. I had feared the truth on her behalf and it had not been my right to make that choice for her. But this was not her way. Her grief was dignified and hidden, as is most grief, which is partly why there is always so much of it to go around.

"I don't know why I'm here," she said.

I didn't know how to respond.

"Just needed to see, you know?"

I looked down at the linoleum.

"No. Course you don't."

She began by telling me that back in that December, a black sedan had driven slowly through town. One of her friends had called her to tell her it was coming. The woman had seen the dress uniform of the man in the passenger seat and she told Mrs. Murphy that the men in the car seemed lost, but that they'd be there soon.

I tried to imagine Mr. and Mrs. Murphy watching from the kitchen window. Snow surely fell as it had fallen all through the evening, over the eaves of the porch and over the hills and lining the branches of the trees. The world clean and obtuse. No angles, nothing hard. The car coming around the last bend in the road, unacknowledged, as if it had not been seen.

Mrs. Murphy and her husband saw the car, to be sure, but some part of it did not register. They stood by the window as if struck by some strange palsy. They were mute and nothing changed in the scene but the snow falling a little harder and the black stain of the car becoming larger as it moved through that blank canvas. And yet they stared. Even when the car stopped in the small turnaround of their drive-way—the idle of the engine soft but undeniable—they did not move. Nor did they move from the window when the captain and chaplain removed their covers and knocked on the door. And despite the fact that the gentle rap of their knuckles asserted the fact that they were truly, wholly real, Mrs. and Mr. Murphy remained looking out the window at the car as if it were one of God's unknowable mysteries.

When the two men gently forced the door open, Mr. Murphy had kissed his wife and put on his hat and coat and left the house out of the back door. When they said to her, "We regret to inform you that your son, Daniel, was killed," she only looked at them with her arms crossed as if wait-ing for some unseen third party to elaborate. None did. The men, fulfilling their obligation with all the grace and defer-ence that men could be asked to, finally left a card in Mrs. Murphy's hand that gave the address of the rooms they'd rented while they waited for a break in the weather. It had a number to call if she had any questions.

As she spoke, I thought of where I had been at that exact moment, but I could not calculate the time difference, nor could I distinguish between all the cold predawn patrols that marked my tour after Murph had died. She said that she'd stood in that same spot for hours. So long in fact that the heat of her body had affected the way the snow collected on the window, leaving the small outline of her figure cleared in the iced-over glass. When she did finally move, it had almost been evening. She walked outside through the still-open back door and found Mr. Murphy there, cross-legged in the snow, which swirled in drifts sometimes up to his waist and collected on his hat and shoulders like a shroud. They sat there together like that in silence. Night began. More fell.

By the time she finished telling me about that day, the coffee had gotten cold, the steam spread out and dissipated above the passing hours. Mrs. Murphy took our mugs and absentmindedly dumped the dregs into a third cup and handed it to me.

"I didn't mean for it all to happen like that," I said.

"Well, what you meant can't do anything now."

"No. You're right."

The army had given up on her eventually, her fight for truth and justice, to know how it was he'd gone from MIA to dead so quickly, why the explanations never fit. But they knew that if they waited long enough people would forget about her pain, and finally a cost-benefit analysis was done and it reached the conclusion that she could now be done away with cheaply. The story of her fight had long since passed from the TV news to tabloid rags, the headlines gaudy and absurd, with pictures of her sitting on a rocking chair, a cigarette dangling from the thin line of her lips. She'd settled for an increase in her SGLI payout and my imprisonment when everyone stopped listening to her, when America forgot her little story, moving as it does so quickly on to other agonies, when even her friends began to smile at her with condescension, saying, "LaDonna, you just gotta find *your* truth in all of this."

That's what she told me anyway. "As if mine's supposed to be different from yours, like you got one and I got another. What the hell's that mean, *your* truth?" she said.

I didn't know. Neither of us said anything for a while and it seemed OK.

"I just wish he hadn't left home," Mrs. Murphy said. She looked at me for a moment. "What about you? You got big plans for getting out?"

"I don't know," I said. I had never really paid attention to where I might end up, which is what I could control, and what mattered. I'd like to think I could choose well if given half a chance. But I had always done something else, always looking back instead on the nothing that remained in memory. I never got it right. All I knew was that I wanted to return to ordinary. If I could not forget, then I'd hope to be forgotten.

I was glad she came. Not because there was any unexpected reconciliation, but because she was tolerant and seemed to want to understand what happened to her son, why I'd made her read a letter that wasn't real, standing in the snow, as I had. I was the last witness to her son's irrevocably human end. He was now just material, but I hardly knew what to make of that. I guess all the words I used to try to explain it to her were like so much straw compared to what I'd seen. But I appreciated the way she reacted to my explanation, as roughly as I told it to her, the connections failing as they did daily on the walls of my cell. I can't quite say what her reaction was exactly; her face still had the dull glow of loss, faded from a feeling always felt toward something else that she would now be forced to measure. Even after talking for six hours straight I couldn't swear to any visible relief. She hadn't offered forgiveness and I hadn't asked for it. But after she left, I felt like my resignation was now justified, perhaps hers too, which is a big step nowadays, when even an apt resignation is readily dismissed as sentimental.

All of that was a long time ago. My loss is fading too and I don't know what it is becoming. Part of it is getting older, I guess, knowing Murph is not. I can feel him getting farther away in time, and I know there are days ahead when I won't think of him or Sterling or the war. For now, though, they've let me out, and I've allowed myself the gift of a quiet quarantine in a cabin in the hills below the Blue Ridge. Sometimes I will smell the Tigris, unchanged forever in my memory, flowing just as it flowed that day, but it is soon replaced by the cold clear air coming down the mountainside between the mezzanines of pines rolling ever upward.

I do feel ordinary again. I guess every day becomes habitual. The details of the world in which we live are always secondary to the fact that we must live in them. So I'm ordinary, except for a few peculiarities that I will probably always carry with me. I don't want to look out over the earth as it unfurls itself toward the horizon. I don't want desert. I don't want prairie and I don't want plains. I don't want anything unbroken. I'd rather look out at mountains. Or to have my view obstructed by a group of trees. Any kind would do: pine, oak, poplar, whatever. Something manageable and finite that could break up and fix the earth into parcels small enough that they could be contended with.

When Murph's mom came to visit she brought me a map of Iraq. I thought it was an odd gesture when I first began to look at it, folding and unfolding it in my cell, struggling with the arrangement of the arbitrary lines that it would fold itself along when I went to put it up at night. Within the map there was a section magnifying Al Tafar and its surrounding landscapes. It stopped being funny after a while. The grid seemed so foreign and imprecise. Just a place scaled out of existence on a map.

The first day in my new cabin I unpacked and laid out a few things on the old olive drab cot I'd bought from the army-navy store outside the base that housed the prison. I didn't have much: some clothes, the map that Mrs. Murphy had given me. I put some tape on the corners and flattened it as best I could against the wall, but the lines of the folds remained. I remember rubbing my finger along one of the creases that ran straight along a very small section of the Tigris. It was the part of the river that ran through Al Tafar. I dug in my bag and found one of my medals and I stuck it in as near as I could figure to the place where we had left him. That map, like every other, would soon be out of date, if it was not already. What it had been indexed to was only an idea of a place, an abstraction formed from memories too brief and passing to account for the small effects of time: wind scouring and lifting the dust of the plains of Nineveh in immeasurable increments, the tuck of a river farther into its bend, hour by hour, year by year; the map would become less and less a picture of a fact and more a poor translation of memory in two dimensions. It reminded me of talking, how what is said is never quite what was thought, and what is heard is never quite what was said. It wasn't much in the way of comfort, but everything has a little failure in it, and we still make do somehow.

I went outside and walked around a bit. It was quiet. I dozed off under the bright sun in the mountains. I heard the rustling of a cloth as it was taken off some small monument in some small corner of America. I heard the soft rustle of other voices, too.

And then I saw Murph as I'd seen him last, but beautiful. Somehow his wounds were softened, his disfigurement transformed into a statement on permanence. He passed out of Al Tafar on the slow current of the Tigris, his body livid, then made clean by the wide-eyed creatures that swam indifferently below the river's placid surface. He held whole even as the spring thaw from the Zagros pushed him farther downstream, passing through the cradle of the world as it greened, then turned to dust. A pair of soldiers watched his passage while resting in the reeds and bulrushes, one calling out to the battered body while the other slept, not knowing Murph was ever one of them, thinking that he must be the victim of another war of which they likely did not feel they were a part, and the voice rose softly through the heat, and it sounded like singing when he said, "Peace out, mother-fucker," loud enough to wake his friend, but the body that he called out to would have been, by then, little more than skeleton, Murph's injuries erased to the pure white of bone. He reached the Shatt al Arab in summer, where a fisher-man who saw him flood into the broad waters where the Tigris and Euphrates marry unknowingly caressed his re-mains with the pole that pushed his small flat-keeled boat along the shallow waters of the marshes. And I saw his body finally break apart near the mouth of the gulf, where the shadows of the date palms fell in long, dark curtains on his bones, now scattered, and swept them out to sea, toward a line of waves that break forever as he enters them.

ACKNOWLEDGMENTS

THIS BOOK WAS primarily written alone. The process of turning those private efforts into what you have just read, however, required many people. Thanks are due, above all, to my mother and father for their endless patience. I've also had extraordinary teachers throughout my life, and many thanks are owed to Patty Strong, Jonathan Rice, Gary Sange, Bryant Mangum, Dean Young and Brigit Pegeen Kelly; your dedication, intelligence and kindness amaze me. I greatly appreciate the opportunity given to me by the Michener Center for Writers, and I'd particularly like to thank Jim Magnuson, Michael Adams and Marla Aiken for their guidance and encouragement. For reading drafts of this novel, and for their friendship, I am indebted to Philipp Meyer, Brian Van Reet, Shamala Gallagher, Virginia Reeves, Ben Roberts, Fiona McFarlane, Caleb Klaces and Matt Greene. Thanks to everyone at Little, Brown, especially Michael Pietsch, Vanessa Kehren, Nicole Dewey and Amanda Tobier.

Thanks also to Drummond Moir and Rosie Gailer at Sceptre. I could not imagine a better group of people to entrust my work to, both at home and abroad. I am also grateful to everyone at Rogers, Coleridge and White for their tireless efforts in getting this book out into the world, especially to Stephen Edwards and Laurence Laluyaux. Lastly, to Peter Straus, it is a privilege. There is nothing else to be said. A complete list of those people to whom I owe a debt of gratitude would be impossible. For this fact alone, I consider myself very lucky.

THE
YELLOW
BIRDS

*A Reading
Group Guide*

Questions and Topics for Discussion

1. Discuss the title, *The Yellow Birds*, and the U.S. Army marching cadence that inspires it. What does the cadence mean to you? How does it, and the title, influence your reading of the book?

2. John Bartle and Murphy first meet when Sergeant Sterling orders them to work together. From that moment on, they spend every minute together. How does their relationship evolve, and how is it shaped by the war? In what ways do you read this as a novel about friendship?

3. The story unfolds in a nonlinear narrative, with scenes alternating between Bartle's time as a soldier at war, and Bartle's time as a veteran. What effect do you think this structure achieves? Do you think the story is better told this way than chronologically? Why or why not?

4. When Bartle returns home, the first person he sees is his mother. How has their relationship changed, and why? What does Bartle's experience reveal about the effect of the war on veterans' families?

5. Bartle believes that cowardice is what motivated him to join the military; he also believes it's what prevents him from becoming a man. When in the novel do you think Bartle is truly a coward, and when do you think he is truly brave? How do you think his notions of cowardice evolve or change throughout the book? And how are they intertwined with his feelings of guilt?

6. 'Nothing seemed more natural than someone getting killed,' Bartle thinks early on in *The Yellow Birds*. What do you make of Bartle's attitude towards death and how does it evolve through the course of the novel?

7. When thinking about the letter he writes to Murphy's mother, Bartle thinks, 'If writing it was wrong, then I was wrong. If writing it was not wrong, enough of what I'd done had been wrong and I would accept whatever punishment it carried.' Why do you think Bartle felt compelled to write the letter? How did it affect Murphy's mother, and how did it affect Bartle? Do you think it was the right decision? Why or why not?

8. In an interview, author Kevin Powers said, 'If I tried to summarize what I was exploring in the book it would be this: what does it mean to try to be good and fail?' Discuss this question with your group. Have you ever

experienced this personally? If so, how did you come to terms with it?

9. In reviews, *The Yellow Birds* has been compared to the works of great writers of war, such as Ernest Hemingway, Erich Maria Remarque, Wilfred Owen, and Tim O'Brien. In O'Brien's work *The Things They Carried*, he writes, 'A thing may happen and be a total lie; another thing may not happen and be truer than the truth.' Discuss your perspective on the intersection of truth and fiction. What truths do you find in *The Yellow Birds*? How does your experience reading fiction about war differ from your experience reading nonfiction accounts, such as newspaper articles?

10. Discuss the ending of the book and your emotional reaction to it. Do you read the ending as melancholy, hopeful, or both? What do you imagine lies ahead for Bartle?

A Conversation with Kevin Powers

How did you come to join the army at the age of seventeen?

I wasn't a particularly good student in high school, but I knew that I wanted to go to college. And given the fact that there is a long tradition of military service in my family, enlisting always seemed like a viable option. It was neither encouraged nor discouraged, but I had by then inferred that the military was where a person went to develop the qualities I had come to admire in my father, my uncle, and both of my grandfathers. The cliché, in my case, was true: I thought that the army would 'make me a man'.

First World War poet Wilfred Owen wrote in the Preface to his poems: 'My subject is War, and the pity of War. The Poetry is in the pity'. Does this apply to *The Yellow Birds*?

I can only say that the impulse to write *The Yellow Birds* came from a desire to look for some truth that I hoped could be found at the core of that most extreme of human experiences. I also thought that by placing the emphasis on the language, using it to demonstrate Bartle's perpetual, unbearable sense of awe and wonder, I'd have at least a chance of connecting to another human being on an emotional level. I wanted to engage with the imagination above all else, because I believe that empathy is an imaginative act.

What sort of reactions have you had from those with combat experience in Iraq?

I don't know that many vets have had a chance to read it yet, but I have had several kind messages of encouragement and support for which I am deeply grateful.

You're also a poet and this comes across in the deeply lyrical quality of your prose. Was this intended in counterpoint to the rawness of the dialogue?

I intended it not just as counterpoint to the rawness of the dialogue, but also to the rawness of the experience. In that respect it is more point than counterpoint. In trying to demonstrate Bartle's mental state, I felt very strongly that the language would have to be prominent. Language is, at its essence, a set of noises and signs that represent what is happening inside our heads. If I have faith that those noises and signs can be received and understood by another person, then I should also have faith that they can be made more finely tuned.

You've said that you were asked most often what it was like in Iraq on your own return. Do you feel that fiction works better than reportage in overcoming people's squeamishness and portraying the reality of combat?

I wouldn't say that it works better, only that it works in a different way. The benefit is that it can confound expectations, particularly in the case of these wars that have been going on so long. It is perfectly understandable that people become inured to the violence when it is presented to them in the same way for ten years or more. Art will sometimes allow you to see the same thing in a new way. But this is only possible because artists don't have the same kind of responsibilities as journalists. The work that journalists do during wartime is utterly essential and, to me, incomprehensibly difficult.

One particularly poignant moment comes when Bartle makes a promise to the mother of his future comrade-in-arms Murphy that he'll make sure her son makes it home safely, by which time in the book we know he will not be able to do. Is Bartle's guilt fuelled more by Murphy's death or his own survival?

I would not be able to separate the two. The root of his guilt is that he wanted to be good, and he tried to be good, but he failed. His conflict is between his desire to redeem that failure and his acceptance of complete powerlessness.

The Yellow Birds has already brought comparison with books as diverse as Erich Maria Remarque's *All Quiet on the Western Front*, Joseph Heller's *Catch-22* and Tim O'Brien's *The Things They Carried*. Were there any particular books that served as an inspiration to you?

Those books were all very meaningful to me. I would include *Meditations in Green* by Stephen Wright, as well as the poetry of Yusef Komunyakaa.

Can you tell us anything about what you're working on at the moment?

I have a collection of poems I'm nearly finished with. And I've begun work on my second novel, about a murder that takes place in Virginia just after the American Civil War.

Interviewed by Jonathan Ruppin of Foyles Bookshops (www.foyles.co.uk)

Kevin Powers on *The Yellow Birds*

The Yellow Birds began as an attempt to reckon with one question: What was it like over there? Sometime in 2007 I thought I might be able to find an answer to that question, not only for the many people who had asked it to me but also for myself. As soon as the first words of the book were put down on the page, I realized I was unequal to the task of answering it, that if there is any true thing in this world it is that war is only like itself.

People, however, are all the same: grief and fear, shame and anger, are as alike in each of us as is our breath or blood, in spite of differences of scope or scale, or the useless divisions between their common or uncommon causes. I hoped that I could begin again with this in mind, understanding now that the difficulty of contending with this question was not that it remained unanswered, but rather how I might find a way to say that the answer could be known to each of us if only we'd allow ourselves to be reminded of it.

Over the course of almost four years I tried to find a way to do this. I started making something like progress that summer of 2007, writing late into the night in my rented room in the Jackson Ward neighborhood of Richmond, Virginia. Sometimes I dedicated whole days of my tenuous employment at a credit card company to furtive work on the novel. I wrote as much as I could whenever I could. I spent the last of those four years stripping away anything and everything that didn't seem essential.

I finished *The Yellow Birds* in Austin, Texas in late September of 2011. What ended then was not just the writing of a book, though it was mostly that, but also something else I had begun seven years before and 7000 miles away from the wooden porch where I went to have a smoke when it was finished. Though I hope I've told one small part of the truth about that war, what I've written is not meant to report or document, nor is it meant to argue or advocate. Instead, I tried with what little skill I have to create the cartography of one man's consciousness, to let it stand, however briefly, as my reminder.